Readers love
ANDREW GREY

Planting His Dream

"I really enjoyed this story and it was very sweet and even the sex scenes were more on the sweet side than being 'hot'"
—Scattered Thoughts and Rogue Words

"Yet again Andrew Grey has managed to capture my imagination by presenting a deceptively simple situation in a light that made it interesting, revealing, and very moving. Bravo!"
—Rainbow Book Reviews

Round and Round

"…this book offered mystery, romance, friendship and a great group of characters."
—Inked Rainbow Reviews

"He built *Round and Round* with suspense, danger, loss and love, and with everlasting friendships and new beginnings."
—The Novel Approach

The Lone Rancher

"This story has an intriguing plot with twists and turns in just about every chapter and was real enough to make it believable… A hot sexy read by the fabulous Andrew Grey."
—Bike Book Reviews

"If you're a fan of Andrew Grey, westerns, sappy romances and the Dreamspun line—you'll enjoy this!"
—The Blogger Girls

More praise for ANDREW GREY

Eyes Only For Me

"A fascinating look deep into the hearts and minds of two men who never expected the discoveries they made along the way of changing and deepening their friendship to the point they become life partners."

—Rainbow Book Reviews

"This is a good story, with well written, well developed characters. There are some seriously hot steamy scenes, and deeply profound dialogue between the main characters…"

—Divine Magazine

The Gift

"Mr. Grey has given us a wonderful story of love and hope and I hope you each grab a copy and enjoy."

—House of Millar

Spirit Without Borders

"Nobody writes like Andrew Grey. I pick up one of his books and start reading, and I can't put it down. This one definitely was one of those books."

—Inked Rainbow Reviews

"The realistic picture Andrew paints about the conditions, the area, the lives of these people grips you and you become emotionally involved in the story and you won't want to put it down until you finish."

—Rainbow Gold Reviews

By ANDREW GREY

Published by
DREAMSPINNER PRESS
www.dreamspinnerpress.com

By ANDREW GREY

Published by
DREAMSPINNER PRESS
www.dreamspinnerpress.com

REKINDLED FLAME

ANDREW GREY

Published by

DREAMSPINNER PRESS

5032 Capital Circle SW, Suite 2, PMB# 279, Tallahassee, FL 32305-7886 USA
www.dreamspinnerpress.com

Rekindled Flame
© 2016 Andrew Grey.

Cover Art
© 2016 L.C. Chase.
http://www.lcchase.com
Cover content is for illustrative purposes only and any person depicted on the cover is a model.

ISBN: 978-1-63477-468-0
Digital ISBN: 978-1-63477-469-7
Library of Congress Control Number: 2016907029
Published June 2016
v. 1.0

Printed in the United States of America
∞

This paper meets the requirements of
ANSI/NISO Z39.48-1992 (Permanence of Paper).

This story is dedicated to the Dreamspinner Press Editorial and Art staff. They all work very hard to take what we write and make it the best it can be. Thank you!

Chapter 1

THE ROAR and screech of the siren faded into the background as the truck slowed to a stop. Morgan popped his seat belt off and jumped down as the wheels quit rolling. Seconds mattered. He'd had that drilled into him since his first day of training, and it was now ingrained into his base personality. He was already pulling hoses off the back of the truck, laying them out as others hooked them up without a word. They knew exactly what to do. They'd practiced so many times they did their jobs without thinking about it.

"The upper floor is nearly completely engulfed. Get some water on it right away," the captain said even as the hose was connected and pressure began to build inside it.

Morgan turned to the group of people gathered in sleepwear toward the back of the lawn, huddled together. He hurried over as soon as the sound of water and fire mixing sent a hiss of steam into the air. "Is everyone out?" he asked them. They looked at each other, stunned.

"Richard isn't here," a kid in blue pajamas answered after a few seconds.

"Oh God," the woman, presumably the mother, groaned. "He lives in the small apartment." She pointed to the side addition of the compact house. "The door is right around the side."

"Thanks, ma'am," Morgan said and hurried back to the captain. "Someone is still inside. The family hasn't seen the tenant, Richard. I'm getting my breathing gear." He didn't wait for an answer as he pulled on a tank and mask with practiced ease. Time was of the essence. Even with the water that was being poured on

1

the structure, the fire was still hot and doing its best to consume the old, dry home. He had a few seconds to ponder just why the house was going up so quickly before he was hurrying up the yard, water running down his suit to give him an initial layer of protection before he went in.

"Shit," he said into his communication system. "There's a ramp." He kicked open the side door. Blinding smoke poured out. Morgan hesitated for a second to give the worst of it the chance to escape before plunging into a world of danger.

The fire roared continually, even though he couldn't see it. The air was hot and getting hotter, which told him the fire was just on the other side of the walls and would most likely break through at any second. He scanned the small living area and then opened the first door he saw. It was empty of anyone as far as he could see. Morgan turned and pushed at another door. It didn't move. Without hesitating, he kicked it, sending the door flying inward.

A man sat in a wheelchair, slumped forward. Morgan had no time to assess his condition. The air was smoky and getting worse.

A crash sounded behind him, and the heat increased. Lights now danced on the walls of the other room. Morgan hefted the man into his arms and over his shoulder. Then he turned and left the room.

Flames crawled across the ceiling, heading for the same door as Morgan. It was a race: him to the exit and the fire to the source of air. Morgan walked as quickly as he could carrying the weight, the flames now racing throughout the room. He knew that within seconds his exit would be closed off.

A figure appeared in the doorway, and water shot to the side and above him, buying Morgan precious seconds that he was able to use to reach the door and safety. He stepped outside and down the ramp, heading right for the first ambulance he saw.

EMTs met him in the yard with a stretcher, and he laid Richard down on it as gently as he could and stepped back, hoping like hell he wasn't too late. Morgan took off his helmet and breathed, taking in cool, clear air. He was sweating like a pig and pulled open the latches of his fire coat to let some of the spring air inside. A bottle of water was shoved into his hand, and he drank without thinking, looking to where he'd left Richard and sighing with relief when he saw him with a breathing mask on. No CPR, just oxygen. He was breathing.

"You did good, again," the captain said, motioning him away from the others. "But this breakneck decision-making of yours has to stop," he added softly. "You ran in there before anyone could assess the situation." A crash interrupted them as the front wall of the home collapsed and fell inward. "You could have been inside."

"So could that man. Instead we're both outside and safe." He and the captain didn't see eye to eye on a number of things, least of which was the speed Morgan thought things needed to be done. The captain was too cautious and lost precious time, in his opinion. But he kept that to himself for now. "You know seconds count. We've all been taught that from day one. I used those seconds to rescue a man in a wheelchair." There was no way the captain could argue with that result.

"All right. It worked out this time, but what if you'd been caught inside?" he countered.

Morgan nodded and went back to work. Having an argument now wasn't going to get him anything, and the captain was worked up enough that if he pressed it, Morgan would find himself in front of the chief once again to explain why he'd done the right thing. It was getting annoying.

He went over to where the EMTs were loading Richard into the back of the ambulance. "Is he going to be all right?"

"He got way too much smoke, but we believe you got to him in time. He's already breathing somewhat better, and he's starting to come around, but he's still groggy and out of it. We're transporting him, but I suspect you saved his life."

"Thanks, Gary." Over time he'd gotten to know most of the ambulance drivers and EMTs. It was a hazard of the profession that their paths crossed too many times. They shook hands, and Morgan turned and went back to where the rest of the guys continued to pour water on what was left of the house, dousing the last of the flames.

By the time they started packing up, the Red Cross had arrived and was meeting with the family. Jackets had been provided, as had water and something to eat. Morgan knew from experience that they'd be helped with temporary shelter as well as given guidance for wading through dealing with insurance and trying to rebuild their lives.

Morgan walked to where they stood.

"Is Richard going to be okay?" the same young boy asked.

"We think so. They're going to take him to the hospital. Is he a family member?" Morgan asked.

"Sort of," the woman said. "He was in the same unit as my brother, Billy, and has been renting the apartment for the last year or so. The kids adore him and call him Uncle Rich, but he isn't a blood relation."

"Billy didn't make it home," the man standing with her explained, and Morgan nodded.

"He'll most likely be taken to Harrisburg Hospital. It's the closest, and they'll do everything they can for him. For now, get yourselves somewhere safe and warm for the night." The kids had to be getting cold in the night air, and he had work he had to do to help the other guys clean up. At times like this, he was never sure what to say, so he tipped his hat and joined the men draining the hoses to load them back on the trucks.

"That was something else," Henry Porter said, smile shining on his smoke-smudged face. "When I saw you coming out of that smoke, it was a damn miracle."

"You got there just in time," Morgan told the younger firefighter, returning his smile. "I wasn't certain I was going to make it until you bought me the time."

"You were going to make it, but I was glad to help." He was all smiles as they rolled up the hoses.

4

"I heard the guy was a veteran," Jimmy Connors said, gathering the nozzles and other equipment. "In a wheelchair."

"Apparently," Morgan said. "It was a good night. Everyone got out." He hated seeing the faces of families who had lost everything. They always seemed so haunted and unsure of what was going to happen next. Morgan had seen that in the family tonight, along with relief that Richard had been rescued safely.

"All right, let's get the last of this packed up so we can go back to the station," the captain called encouragingly, and their talking ceased as they all got to work. What could be pulled out and put to use in a matter of minutes always took much longer to stow and get ready for the next time it was needed. When the equipment was stowed and the area cleaned up, they climbed into the trucks and quietly went back to the station.

Morgan dragged himself off the truck. The energy that had sustained him at the fire and through the rescue had now deserted him, and all he wanted was to climb into a bed. Working late when most people are asleep was the hardest part of this job for him. Morgan was a morning person. At home he was usually up early, always had been, so working late into the night went counter to his natural rhythm.

"Let's get the hoses set to dry and call it a night. The rest can wait," the captain said, and the men got to work and then headed inside and up to the dormitory. They often worked long shifts, and catching a few hours' sleep was always a godsend. Some of the guys would sit at the table and play cards or talk through the entire shift. Not Morgan. He headed right up and took his turn in the bathroom, then collapsed on one of the narrow beds, letting oblivion take over for a little while.

He only slept for a few hours, just long enough to recharge his batteries, and then he was up once again, helping to prepare the equipment for the next call, which they all knew could come at any moment.

"What will you do now that your rotation is over and you have some time off?" Henry asked without looking up from where he was cleaning the side of the pumper. The younger man's enthusiasm always seemed to run over the brim.

"I don't know. Probably sleep for a while, and then...." That was always the part of that answer that vexed him. Outside of work he didn't have much of a life.

"Will you go out, find someone to keep you company?" Henry waggled his eyebrows and reminded Morgan just how young Henry was and how old he seemed to be getting. "There are some great clubs downtown, and the girls would be more than interested, if you know what I mean. They love firemen."

"Is that why you became one?" Morgan asked. He was only giving Henry a hard time. Being a firefighter had to be in your blood or you didn't last very long. The job demanded a lot, physically, personally. It tended to take over and become what your life—well, at least his life—revolved around. Relationships suffered, and most went by the wayside over time.

"You know it's not," Henry answered seriously. "But it is one of the perks of the job."

Morgan paused. "You know you aren't likely to see me in one of those particular clubs." Morgan had decided some years earlier that he wasn't going to hide who he was.

"I thought that was only rumor and such." Henry looked him over. "You don't look like you're... that way." From what Henry had said and the way he'd talked sometimes, Morgan figured Henry had come to them straight off a rural Lancaster farm.

"Gay people come in all shapes and sizes, and believe it or not, we can do just about anything."

Henry's gaze drifted to the floor, hand stopping for a second. "I didn't mean anything by it. I guess you're just the first gay person I've met." He continued working.

"I don't think so. You remember Angus, the man who came in at the last training session talking about how fires start? He has a partner who isn't a woman. They've been together about a year now, I guess. His name's Kevin, and he's really nice."

"You know them?"

"I've met Kevin one time." Morgan didn't want to go into how all gay people didn't necessarily know each other. It wasn't his job to educate the kid, nor was it wise to try to pop too many of his bubbles all at once. "You okay?"

"Yeah," Henry answered quickly.

Morgan knew he was covering some discomfort, and Morgan figured that was okay. "If you've got questions, ask."

Henry wiped faster and faster. Soon Morgan figured either his arm was going to fall off or he was going to rub right through the red paint.

"There's no reason to be upset or nervous."

He finally stopped and set down the rag, working his arm in a circle because he must have made it sore. "But what if...." He stopped and shook his head. "I'm being dumb, right?"

"Maybe a little?" Morgan teased. "Now get back to work, and try not to rub all the paint off." He picked up another rag and helped the kid. Polishing was one of the most detailed and mind-numbing jobs, and usually it fell to the newbies. Morgan never minded it, and he could help the kid out. They were all a team.

Once his shift was over a few hours later, Morgan gathered his things to get ready to leave. There had been no further calls, and turnover to the morning shift had been completed. "You working today too?" Morgan asked Henry when he didn't seem to be getting ready to go.

"They're a man short, and I volunteered. They need the help, and I can use the hours."

"Don't wear yourself out. This job is a marathon that can last a long time." He clapped the young firefighter on the shoulder.

"Don't worry," Phillips, one of the senior firefighters, said. "We'll make sure he gets rest."

Morgan nodded and hefted his bag. "Are you going somewhere in particular?" Henry asked, following him out.

"Yeah, I'm going to stop at the hospital to see how the man I helped last night is doing, and then I'm going home." Morgan headed for the door and threw his bag into the trunk of his car before pulling out and driving across town to a place he knew way too well.

Morgan had saved a number of people over the years. It was one of the things that went with the job. Not getting there in time could rip a firefighter apart, and saving someone brought you a kinship no one else could understand. All he knew about this man was that his name was Richard, but in a few minutes they had shared something unique. Morgan had had an influence on the rest of Richard's life.

"Can I help you?" the woman behind the visitors' desk asked as he approached. "Oh, hi, Morgan," she said when she recognized him. "What can I do for you?"

"There was a man brought into emergency last night. His first name was Richard. I need to know what room he's in."

"You don't want much," she told him and began typing. Geri was used to his unorthodox inquiries. She was a little younger than him and had worked at the hospital for years. "What happened to him?"

"I got him out of a burning building last night, and I want to make sure he's okay." He leaned against the counter, relaxing while she searched.

"I found him. Room 212. It says he can receive visitors."

She handed him a pass, and Morgan thanked her before striding toward the elevators. He rode to the second floor and then walked through familiar hallways to the ward and down to Richard's room. He paused outside and heard nothing. Peering in, he saw a sleeping figure in the bed. Maybe he'd come too early. He walked in anyway and stood by the end of the bed.

"Who are you?" Richard demanded in a rough voice that set Morgan on alert.

"I'm the firefighter who pulled you out last night. I just wanted to make sure you were okay."

"You rescued me from the fire?" he asked. "You should have saved your efforts and left me there. Everyone would be so much better off." The anger and vitriol rolled off him in a tidal wave of blackness.

"Well, I did," Morgan said as he put his jacket on the nearby chair. "The kids were worried about you."

That softened some of Richard's features as a nurse came rushing into the room. "Mr. Smalley, you need to remain calm." She helped him to lie back down, glaring at Morgan. "His breathing needs to be as regular as possible to give him time to heal."

Morgan barely heard her. He stared at the man in the bed and let her do her job. Once she left, he moved closer.

"Richard Smalley? Did you grow up on a farm outside Enola?" Even before Richard spoke, Morgan knew the answer.

"Yes." Richard lifted his head of sandy-blond hair, the color of perfectly ripe corn. Morgan knew that color so well, even after all these years.

"It's Morgan, Morgan Ayers. We were friends when we were growing up." He continued staring at the man Richie had become. "What were we, thirteen the last time we saw each other?"

"Yeah. After seventh grade when your dad moved the two of you away. Where did you go? I went away to summer camp, and when I came back you'd moved."

Morgan nodded. "Dad lost his job and got a new one in Detroit, so he packed us up and we moved. Not that we stayed there for very long either. After that we were in Cleveland, and then Pittsburgh, where Dad finally stopped drinking and we could settle down. He remarried, and that's where I spent my last few years of high school." God, he wanted to hurry forward and give Richard a hug, but he didn't have the right any longer. It had been decades, but Morgan had never forgotten Richie. How could he? "I wrote you, but I was thirteen and…."

"Yeah. It wasn't like there was Facebook back then."

Richard was definitely happier than he'd been, with a hint of the smile Morgan remembered from his friend. The memories had dulled over time as the years had gone by, but Morgan would never forget Richie, no matter how long he lived. That wasn't possible. How did you forget the one person you told your deepest, darkest secrets to, and he'd not only understood but told you his in return? How did you forget the boy who had made things better and brought you home when your dad drank most of the grocery money away? Richie had been the one who'd helped see that he didn't starve more times than he wanted to remember.

"You're a firefighter?" Richie asked. "You always said that was what you wanted to be when you grew up, even back then."

"Yeah, and it's a good thing I was, because I hauled you out of the bedroom last night."

"I thought I was dead. I got so disoriented I thought the bedroom door was the way out, and then after that I didn't have the lung power to do anything else. The door closed, and that's the last thing I remember."

"I broke it down and got you out of there, carried you out over my shoulder." He pulled the chair closer to the bed, moved his jacket, and sat down. "You were out of it, but I got you out in time, and once they get the smoke out, you should be good to go."

Richie yanked the covers to the side. "I'll never be good to go again, Morgan." He looked down at his legs. "The best I can do is wheel myself around, but I'm assuming my chair got fried."

"Along with everything else, I'm afraid. The fire was really hot, and I got you out just before it broke through. Damn thing chased me to the door." He wished he had better news.

"Did everyone else get out?" Richie asked.

"Yeah. They were pretty shaken up, and the Red Cross was helping them. But they were all okay."

"I served with Grace's brother in Iraq," Richie said.

"You always wanted to be a soldier," Morgan said. "Marine?"

"Yeah."

Richie looked totally pained, and he had to be wearing out. There were so many questions Morgan wanted to ask, but Richie was fading, and wearing him out wasn't going to do any good.

"I think I'm getting tired."

Morgan nodded and was about to stand up.

"You aren't going to disappear for a few decades again, are you?" Richie asked.

"No. I'm going to head home to get some rest since I just got off shift, but I'll stop by later today to make sure you're doing okay, and we can talk some more." Morgan stood and found a pen and pad on the tray. He jotted down his number for Richie. "I'll see you later."

They shared a smile, and then Richie's eyes drifted closed, so Morgan left the room.

He walked back through the hospital hallways in a slight daze, unable to believe he'd found his friend after all these years. By the time he made it to the exit, he was grinning like an idiot, and his spirit felt lighter than it had in a very long time. He had no logical reason to feel that way. But it didn't seem to matter.

He drove home humming to himself. He was fucking *humming*. Morgan rarely hummed, sang, or whistled. He turned on the radio, and within moments he was singing along with the music. By the time he got home, Morgan was damn near giddy. And he was never that happy or excited about much of anything. God, he was so pathetic. He worked, took care of his home, worked some more, and slept. That was his life, and it had been that way for so long he couldn't remember anything different.

Since he was a municipal employee of Harrisburg, he was required to live in the city. Luckily years ago he'd been able to buy a house in the Italian Lake neighborhood. It was one of the nicer areas of the city. He pulled his car into the garage and hoisted his bag of gear out of the trunk before heading inside.

Morgan dropped his gear in the foyer and continued on through the house, where he checked the mail and took a few minutes to answer some e-mails before heading to the bathroom.

A shower, comfortable clothes, and a light blanket later, he was curled on the sofa, watching television and trying to relax. But all he kept thinking of was Richie and wondering what he'd been through. To say that Richie had been through a lot had to be an understatement. He knew there was something traumatic behind his inability to walk, but there was more than that. His reaction told Morgan that Richie didn't think he had much to live for, and that was really sad, because the Richie he remembered was pretty damned special.

"WE'RE GOING to play wedding," Amy announced in her authoritative—okay, bossy—way, glaring at both of them as she pulled open the barn door on her parents' farm.

Morgan trudged inside with Richie next to him. They shared a concerned glance. The last thing either of them wanted to play was wedding, but Amy's family had ponies, and they wanted the chance to ride, so they'd put up with just about anything.

"I'm going to be the preacher, because ladies can be preachers now, and Morgan, you're the groom." Amy didn't say any more, but she glared at Richie, because that meant he'd have to be the bride.

Poor Richie groaned and took a step back. "I'm not being a girl." He crossed his arms over his chest, glaring right back at Amy.

She sighed loudly in that way she had. Morgan crossed his arms as well for good measure, because he wasn't being the girl either. Even though he was willing to put up with a lot for the chance to ride a pony, this was approaching the breaking point.

"You don't have to wear a dress, but somebody has to be the bride. Now come on."

She led them up the stairs to a landing below the hayloft where the stairs split in two directions like the barn version of a grand staircase. Only this one was raw wood covered in bits of hay and dust. Still, the ceiling towered over them, giving the scene a sense of grandeur that was of course lost on his thirteen-year-old self.

"Okay. I'm going to stand here, and you two stand right there."

She had them face each other. Morgan could tell Richie was nervous, but he went along. Maybe once this was over and Amy was happy, they could ride and forget all about this wedding nonsense.

"There, that's it," she said when she was happy. She cleared her throat and took her place.

"Amy," Richie began. "We didn't come here for this, and it's getting hot." He pulled at the collar of his shirt. Amy had insisted they button up their collars because they were supposed to be wearing tuxedos. But the barn was stifling, and up here toward the loft it was even hotter.

Amy cleared her throat again, pretending to open a book. "Dearly beloved, we are gathered together to join Morgan and Richie in holy matrimony."

Dang it if she didn't have all the words memorized.

"Marriage is a sacred institution brought forth by God." She went on a minute and then stepped forward. "Do you, Richie, take Morgan to be your husband?" Amy asked and giggled. "You have to say 'I do.'"

"I do," Richie said, and then Amy turned to Morgan with too big a smile.

"Do you, Morgan, take Richie to be your husband?"

She was clearly enjoying this, and Morgan tried to think of things he could do to get even with her, if only for appearance's sake.

"I do," Morgan answered—mainly in order to get this over with, but secretly he liked the idea of Richie as his husband.

At Amy's insistence, they exchanged rings. They were nails that had been bent into ring shapes. She pressed one into each of their hands, and they put them on each other.

"I now pronounce you husband and husband."

She broke down into giggles again, and for a second Morgan stared into Richie's eyes before they both backed away.

"Let's do something else," Richie said.

"You invited us over to ride ponies," Morgan challenged Amy. "Were you lying?"

"No. Mama will be out in a little while, and she said she'd take us all for a ride," Amy said with her nose in the air.

"Amy, boys," Amy's mother called, and they hurried down the stairs to where she stood in boots and helped them saddle the ponies. "You can all ride in the ring out back."

She led them out one by one, and Morgan happily rode a pony for the first time in his life.

MORGAN WOKE with a start, trying to remember where he was. He was an adult, not thirteen years old. He remembered the wedding. After riding for about an hour, they had gotten off the ponies and helped brush the animals. He smiled as he remembered how he and Richie had forced Amy to a vow of silence. Neither of them wanted this to get back to school.

He sat up and blinked, checking the time and turning his attention to whatever was on television. Part of him wondered if he'd dreamed the whole thing, but Morgan knew most of what had appeared in his dream had indeed happened, many years earlier. He checked his phone and found he'd received a call and had a voice mail. It was Richie.

"They are going to release me from the hospital this afternoon. I didn't want you to visit and not find me." There were hems and haws. "Thanks for saving me."

Morgan hung up and stared at his phone. This was a moment of decision, and Morgan pushed aside the blanket, hurried into jeans and a T-shirt, pulled on a pair of shoes, and then ran out the door to his car. He rushed to the hospital, swearing when he had to stop at each light. Finally he arrived and caught an elevator to the second floor. He half expected to find room 212 empty, but Richie sat on the edge of the bed wearing jeans and a flannel shirt that hung on him, probably from a donation bin.

"I didn't mean for you to run down," Richie said. "I didn't want you visiting when I wasn't going to be here."

"Where are you going to go?" Morgan asked.

"Some people from the Red Cross said they were going to put me up in a hotel for the week, and some people here at the hospital banded together to get me a chair, so I was going to go there."

"No. It's nice that they've got you a chair, but I have room, and you can come stay with me. The house is on one level, and we can figure out how to get you where you need to be. You can't go to a hotel." That just wasn't something he could let happen to his old friend. "When will you be able to go?"

"The doctor needs to sign the discharge, and then I can leave."

Morgan got the wheelchair that was sitting in the corner. It wasn't new, but it was serviceable, and he wheeled it over to Richie and lifted him down into it. "I should have asked if you wanted to wait on the bed."

"No. I'm used to being in a chair." He sounded about as thrilled as if he were saying he was going to the dentist for a root canal. "I hate them. The entire time I'm in this damn thing my head screams that I'm not what I was."

"Want to tell me what happened?" Morgan offered.

"Fuck no. I've done way too much talking about it to too many people. Everyone says if you talk about it, you'll feel better," he mocked. "All it fucking does is make you relive the worst shit in your life, and who wants that?"

"Okay. Then tell me about your family. Are your mom and dad still alive?"

"No. They lasted about six months after all this shit. I was in one of those veterans' facilities where they put the angry and nearly dead. It was one of those facilities that were on the news all the time because it was complete crap. They came for a visit and were driving back." Richie lowered his gaze. "Dad was too tired, and he ran off the road. I don't know what they were thinking. Dad and Mom were past seventy, and they drove down to the DC area every week to see me." He turned away. "That's enough of this crap. How's your dad?"

"He's doing well. I swear sometimes he's going to outlive us all. He's in Florida now and seems happy. He remarried, and my stepmother is okay, but she makes Dad happy, so that's what really matters."

"There's a but there somewhere," Richie prompted.

"She doesn't approve of some of what she sees as the choices I made in my life. Not that it really matters. She and I aren't particularly close, and when I call she says hello briefly and then passes the phone to my dad who, believe it or not, is easygoing and doesn't let things bother him. We talk, and he tells me about what he and Lydia are doing. I know more about where they went to eat on a daily basis than I do about the dinner I had last night."

"So you're a fireman," Richie said when the conversation petered out after a few minutes.

Morgan had wondered what it would be like to see Richie again after all these years, but this was never what he'd pictured.

"I love it. The hours can be horrendous, but I like helping people, and there's a huge rush when you're at a fire. The adrenaline pumps, and you have to be on your toes. Split-second decisions that can mean the difference between life and death. I thought about going into the service the way you did, but I was already out, and at that time DADT was in force, and I couldn't do that, so I went a different way."

"Mr. Smalley," a woman said as she came into the room. "I have a few forms for you to sign, and then you should be free to go."

She handed Richie a clipboard, and he signed. Morgan waited for him to get his things and then realized he probably didn't have any. What little Richie had was gone in the fire.

"That's it?" he said as he handed the clipboard back.

"Yes."

She turned and left, and Richie sat still, staring at nothing.

"That's it. I have nothing, am nothing, and have nowhere to go. I've hit the complete and total bottom of the barrel."

He turned away to look out the window, and Morgan watched as Richie bowed his head.

"Let's get out of this place. It's depressing," Morgan said as he gripped the handles of Richie's chair. As he was about to turn him, an orderly came in and took control of it.

"Ready to go, sir?" he asked in a bright tone.

"Ready as I'll ever be," Richie said, and the orderly wheeled Richie out of the room.

As they walked down the hospital corridors, Morgan wondered what would have happened if he hadn't stopped in and recognized Richie. Would he have ended up on the street somewhere? It was clear that the people who had been taking care of him weren't able to do that any longer now that their home was gone as well. Things happen for a reason.

"I'll bring my car around," Morgan said when they reached the hospital doors. He hurried across the lot and brought his car up under the portico. The orderly helped Richie get in, and Morgan placed the chair in the trunk. He waved and got in the car.

"You can drop me anywhere you want," Richie said. "I can take care of myself."

"Okay," Morgan answered and put the car in gear.

He had a number of stops he wanted to make, and the first one was Target. Richie grumbled when Morgan pushed him to the personal care aisle and told him to get what he needed. The protestations grew louder when they reached the clothing section.

"Just get what you need and stop bitching," Morgan snapped. "You can pay me back if you want, but you need things, so quit the griping and just say thank you."

"You're bossier than my drill sergeant," Richie countered.

"And you're a pain in the ass." Morgan glared at his childhood friend. "Now that we have that out of the way, get some pants, shirts, and underwear. Regardless of how you feel, you need some basic things, so pick them out. I know you have your pride, but you lost everything in a fire yesterday. There's no shame in accepting help from an old friend."

Richie hesitated. "As long as you let me pay you back."

"Fine," Morgan agreed, and Richie propelled himself in the department, choosing a few things. Once he knew Richie's size, Morgan added a few others, and they wheeled up to the checkout. The purchases were rung up, and Morgan put the amount on a credit card.

"I will pay you back for all this," Richie reiterated as he wheeled himself back out toward the car with Morgan carrying the bags. "I hate this," Richie commented as soon as he was buckled in the seat. "It sucks being dependent on other people all the time."

"You know that's bullshit, man. You can be as independent as you want to be. They can fit cars with hand controls, and you have a brain, so you can get a job. The Marines have to have left you with skills, and you were always smart."

"I was working at home, helping people maintain their websites. But the computer went up in the flames. Stuff was backed up to the cloud, but I can't afford to get a new one right now. Between that and my disability benefits from the service, I was barely making ends meet, and now I need to find a new place to live. I have an old car fitted with hand controls that I hope wasn't burned in the fire."

"Okay. We can check that out later, and I have my older laptop. I got a new one last year after the old one crashed. It's been rebuilt, and it's blank, so we can set it up, and you can use that one." That was an easy problem solved. "I have good Wi-Fi, so you should be able to get online."

"I can't take any more from you," Richie said.

"You need a chance to get yourself together, and the computer is just sitting there. You may as well use it." He drove down Second Street and continued to the north end of the city, weaving through the neighborhood until he pulled into his driveway. "I don't have a ramp, so I'll need to help you get in and out for now." Morgan got out and retrieved Richie's chair. He wanted to let him get out of the car on his own, so Morgan grabbed the bags and hurried up to the door, taking the things inside to set them down. Then he returned and got Richie backed up the stairs and into the kitchen. "If we need to move furniture to make things easier, let me know. Your room is down the hall on the left. The bathroom is on the right, and the door should be wide enough for you to get in. Everything is pretty much a straight shot here, so it should be okay."

Richie slowly wheeled out of the kitchen, and Morgan put things away and set Richie's clothes and things on his bed.

"You have a nice place, Morgan."

"It's home. I bought it a few years ago. It was hard saving for the down payment, but I managed. Are you hungry?"

"No. Just tired."

"You want to sit on the sofa or lie down on the bed?" Morgan headed toward him, but Richie had already transferred himself to the sofa. Morgan handed him the remote and sat in his favorite chair, putting his feet up. He was tired and closed his eyes.

Morgan woke to a bloodcurdling scream that shook the house. He jumped up, instantly on alert. Richie thrashed on the sofa, rolling back and forth. Morgan raced over to prevent him from falling off onto the floor. "Richie," he cried. He managed to catch him before he hit the floor. The rolling was bad enough, but as soon as he touched Richie, he began to thrash and fight. "It's me. You're safe. It's Morgan. We were kids together, remember?" He was running out of things to say when Richie opened his eyes, and Morgan was able to settle him back on the cushions. "You're okay. No one is going to hurt you."

"Morgan?" Richie asked tentatively, breathing hard and then starting to cough.

Morgan did his best to calm him down. He knew breathing evenly and regularly was the primary thing Richie needed in order to heal.

"It's me. You're safe here. This is my house."

Richie nodded and lay on his back. "I was back there, in the battle."

"That's what I thought. Does that happen often?" Morgan asked.

"Yeah. Most nights I wake up shaking. Sometimes I go right back to sleep, and other times it's like that, where I'm back there and can't get out. People say you relive the bad parts, but my dreams are different each time. They change and become worse sometimes." He closed his eyes once again. "I'm sorry for doing this to you." He sat up and pulled his chair closer. "You should just let me go. I'm not any use to anyone. I tried to get a real job but couldn't hold it. The last boss I had, I threatened to break his neck because he made me angry. That's why I do this web work. It isn't like punching a clock, and when I'm not feeling too well, I can lay off for a day or so." He was still breathing too hard.

"Lay back and rest awhile. You got yourself worked up, and your lungs are going to make you pay for it unless you relax." He got Richie to settle again.

"I really should go. I'm not good for you... or anyone."

"Why don't you let me decide what's good for me and relax? You're fine, and it was only a little yelling." Richie wasn't so heavy or big that Morgan couldn't hold his own. He was starting to wonder how well Richie had been eating lately. "I want you to feel safe." Morgan smiled when Richie looked his way. "I know we haven't seen each other in a very long time, but I'm still your oldest friend."

"How can you do this? Take in a near total stranger."

"You're aren't a stranger. You're my husband."

He got a blank look that bordered on insane.

"Remember, we were thirteen years old, and Amy married us in her barn? We wanted to ride ponies, and she dragged us along to do what she wanted."

Richie put his arm over his eyes. "That was real? I thought it was some demented delusion that popped into my head along with the flashbacks and nightmares."

"It really happened," Morgan said. "We did everything together. Remember when we were eleven and your mom and dad took us camping?"

"It rained almost the entire week, and we spent way too much time inside that little camper trying to keep dry."

"Yeah, but when the rain let up, we'd bound outside and race through the woods. Remember when we found those frogs and brought them back?" Morgan asked. "You handed one to your mom, and she dang near freaked out. Your dad laughed so hard he fell off the picnic table bench. She was so mad at us. Well, mostly at your dad for laughing."

"It was a big frog."

"Then the day the rain stopped and the sun came out—it was like we won the lottery. Your dad took us hiking, and your mom went into town and brought back a whole bunch of soda. We went swimming and played the entire day." Morgan could remember that as clear as if it were yesterday. "That was one of the best times of my childhood, rain and all."

"I remember you didn't want to go home, and I didn't understand why. I do now, though. Your dad was drinking so much, and you were never sure what you were going to walk into."

"Nope. It was the best week because I didn't have to worry about Dad passing out and me trying to make sandwiches for dinner when there wasn't anything in the house. I swear your mom fed me more than my dad did."

"What happened after you moved?"

"I made do as best I could until we got to Pittsburgh. A neighbor kept turning my dad in. He was so angry, but they finally said they were going to take me away if he didn't get help. I figured I was going to live with strangers, but my dad went into treatment that they arranged, and he got better and stopped drinking. Then our lives improved and he started acting like a dad again. But that was five years after we left. I was so skinny and small from not always getting enough to eat. At school I used to wolf down the food at lunch because it was free, and sometimes I hadn't eaten since the day before."

"I didn't know," Richie said.

"I'm pretty sure your mom did, though. I remember she used to always have a few presents for me at Christmas. That last year she gave me a truck and a shirt and pair of pants. Those were the clothes I wore when I went back to school. That year my dad slept most of Christmas day. I don't remember what I got from him, but it wasn't much. Your mom gave me my Christmas." Morgan sat back down. "I know we left in a hurry, but I was able to say good-bye to her, and she promised she'd tell you what happened."

"Jesus," Richie said. "I had no idea."

"You were a kid, and so was I. Neither of us knew any different. Things were the way they were, and we made the best of it." Things were very hard after they moved away. They'd left the people who had been supporting him for the past few years, and until his father got help, Morgan had been pretty much on his own. "What happened to you after I left?"

"I'd lost my best friend, but I continued on, I suppose. Things weren't the same. We used to do everything together, and I never had a friend like that again until I was in the Corps. The men in my unit were my brothers, and the only reason I knew how to behave was because I'd had a brother before—you." Richie slowly sat back up. "You remember when we were thirteen, just a few weeks before I was supposed to go to camp? You told me your greatest secret."

"That I liked boys. I know. At the time it seemed so groundbreaking to tell someone."

"Yeah, and I said I was the same way. We kept each other's secrets."

"We did more than that. We were part of each other," Morgan said. He was probably being stupid, but he couldn't help wondering if it was possible to know the one person who was the other half of your soul at thirteen years of age. At the time, moving had nearly torn him apart. He couldn't tell Richie how he'd thought his heart would be ripped in half as his father gathered him into the car that last morning and then drove away. Morgan hadn't been able to look at the house that Richie had lived in because he'd have cried, and if he'd done that, his father would have gotten angry.

Morgan stood. He needed to get these silly notions out of his head. He was no longer a child. Both he and Richie were men now, and it was time to stick to realistic notions and to see life for what it was: a nearly endless stream of disappointments broken up by the occasional spot of brightness. "I got some chicken for dinner. I know it won't be like your mom's, but it's the best I can do." He turned on the television to give them something to watch rather than spending their time going down depressing memory lane.

Chapter 2

"How on earth did Morgan find me again after all these years?" Richie asked himself as he tried to get his head around the fact that when he'd lost everything, it had been Morgan who'd rescued him from the burning building, even though he didn't remember, and now Morgan had taken him in. What was even more remarkable was that Morgan looked every bit the part of a firefighter rescuer. He was nothing like the thin, wiry boy he'd known when they were kids. There were moments when his smile or the way he bit his upper lip when he was thinking hearkened back to the boy he knew, but mostly this was someone he didn't recognize.

Morgan was tall, broad, and strong. He did have the same intense eyes and jet black hair. It wasn't as though he doubted Morgan was who he claimed, but Richie didn't recognize this person. That is, until he took that trip down memory lane. Once they grew quiet and the fatigue caught up with him once again, he dozed off.

Richard hated sleeping. It was when the memories he'd spent four years trying to run away from caught up with him. During the day he could keep them away—life kept them at bay. Someone had called sleep a minideath or something. Well, for him it was true. Death and destruction haunted and plagued his dreams. He knew them well. Richard had met them up close and personal, and they'd left their scars on both his body and mind.

This time on Morgan's sofa was different. When he dozed off, they stayed away. He had no doubt they'd return, but for now, this afternoon, he was on a huge beach in a bathing suit. His was green, and Morgan's was red. His friend carried water in a container so big he rocked back and forth with each step. It had a spout on it, and Morgan set it at the top of the incline. Then the two of them dug a small hole and began digging a raceway for the water to follow back to the lake. All around them were people talking and kids laughing. "Are you ready?" Morgan asked, scurrying up to where Richard was putting the finishing touches on the raceway.

"Almost," Richard said, hurrying excitedly to finish the bend in the raceway. He handed Morgan a large rock. "Use that as a dam right there. If we got the angle right, it could act like a waterfall on the downward side. That will be cool."

Morgan dug where he indicated and placed the rock. When Richard finished, he helped, and when everything was ready, Richard turned on the water. It filled the initial pool and then spilled out, running slowly down the raceway, around the various bends and up to the rock dam. It filled the lake behind and then reached the top and spilled over, continuing down. Richard turned to Morgan, who was grinning, and watched as he raced toward him. Suddenly Morgan clutched his chest, smile fading, fingers covered in blood. He gasped and fell to his knees before collapsing onto the ground. Richard stood helpless as the raceway flowed red down to the lake.

He woke with a gasp, sitting up, looking at the grown-up Morgan as he tried to inhale. It was a dream, another reminder of how messed up and freaky his mind worked now. Thankfully Morgan smiled at him and turned back to the television. "You have to be hungry."

"I guess I am." He willed the residual images from his mind. "I hate that I can't remember anything without my thoughts getting all twisted up."

"Let me guess. You start out down a normal path and suddenly you're back on the battlefield or it turns gruesome," Morgan said, and Richard wondered how he knew. "I've taken classes. First thing, because we have to deal with losing people under traumatic, stressful situations, and there are times when we deal with someone who's in a fire but thinks they're back on the battlefield. Stress can do some wild things to people, so we have to be trained for anything."

"I was starting to think you were reading my mind." He stopped short of telling Morgan about his dream. It usually didn't go over too well when he told someone he'd dreamed their death.

"Nope. Figured you were having some sort of flashback." Morgan hoisted himself out of the chair. "You want to help with dinner? You're welcome to stay where you are."

Richard shook his head and pulled his chair over, shifting his weight so he could get into it. "I need to do something or I'll end up sitting around all day." He followed Morgan into the kitchen. The counters were too high for him to work comfortably, so he slid up to the table. Morgan brought over the stuff for a fresh salad, and Richard got to work chopping and cutting.

"Geez, you're good at that," Morgan said, and when Richard was done, Morgan brought over some onions, chicken, and vegetables. "I'm going to make a stir fry."

"No worries. Give me a few minutes." He chopped everything into regular-shaped cubes and passed the board back to Morgan. "I had intended to work in a kitchen, but it turned out that putting a guy who had regular flashbacks around sharp knives and open flame wasn't such a good idea." Thankfully he hadn't hurt anyone, but the job hadn't lasted very long after he'd had an episode that involved him throwing a knife with perfect accuracy across the kitchen because he thought one of the other men might have been the enemy. "Turned out a lot of the jobs I've tried to take haven't been a real good fit." He backed away from the table as Morgan put rice on to cook.

"How long were you on active duty?" Morgan asked.

"I went into the Corps right out of high school." Richard set down his knife. "The other guys in basic training used to look at me sideways because I wasn't this huge guy. But I showed them very quickly. I had worked on farms the entire time I was in high school, and that builds strength, so in a way I was ahead of a lot of the other men. A Marine is built by the Corps from the boots up, and I had already started some of that, at least physically. I flew through basic training and was assigned to duty in Iraq. It was supposed to be peacekeeping." Richard grew quiet. "To answer your question, I was in the Corps almost ten years and had considered making it my career."

"I see," Richard said.

"No you don't. In civilian life, if I was injured like this, they'd be expected to find a place for me. I have skills and knowledge that could be very useful to the Corps, but they took one look at my injury, mustered me out, and said have a nice fucking day. I was given a medical discharge and benefits and chucked the hell aside. I can get medical help for the rest of my life if I want to deal with the fucking VA, which is a huge bureaucracy filled with paperwork on top of paperwork. No one wants to work for them. There are good doctors there, but they're few and far between. The good ones leave because they can't take all the crap any longer. It isn't like I can take my VA benefits and go anywhere like normal insurance." He knew he was talking way too loudly. "I have to get lost in their system and shuffled around." He pounded the arms of the chair. The anger welled up and washed over him like a bath in dark, thick oil. "The people here were the nicest I've had in a while. I thought if I came home that I might be able to rebuild my life. It hasn't worked out that way."

"What about the people you were living with?"

"The Thompsons? Grace is such a good person. I served with her brother until he was killed." Richard shook his head. "He was my best friend, and we got leave together, so when we came home, he met my folks, and I met his sister. I think Billy had this idea that if he introduced me to her, we'd hit it off. She'd gone through a rough divorce then."

"So you never told him?" Morgan asked.

"I didn't tell anyone. I loved being a Marine, and they took that 'don't tell' stuff very seriously. I kept quiet about sex completely. I was like a monk for years and kept that part of myself locked away." Richard wheeled around. "You have no idea how hard that was."

"I suppose it was."

"It wasn't being around the guys. I never had thoughts for them. They were my brothers, and it would have felt weird to be involved with them. But on leave or when I was off base, I felt free and would sometimes go to places where I could meet men. It was liberating, and I was strong and good looking, so I attracted attention. But after a day or so, it was back to real life, and I'd leave it behind and go to work."

"That sounds pretty lonely," Morgan said.

"It was and it wasn't. I was closer to some of these guys than they were to their wives. There wasn't sex, but that was about all. I knew when they weren't feeling well by the look in their eyes. I knew if they weren't eating or drinking enough. I knew when Tommy Cripton's wife had a baby before her parents because we were watching the video feed of the birth right along with him. These men were my family, but when they discharged me, they yanked all that away." Richard blinked a few times. Until he said those words, he hadn't realized exactly what had happened.

"And then your parents were killed and you were all alone," Morgan added, and Richard nodded.

"So you're pretty much caught up on my life over the past twenty years. I've seen parts of the world few people get to see, and mostly I wish I could forget all about them. What I want more than anything is to try to get my life back, but it seems the dreams and memories are in control more than I am."

"You know they'll always be with you, and they won't just go away. The best you can hope for is to learn to live with them." Morgan stopped and turned back to the stove. "Sorry, that sounded preachy as hell."

"It's true, though. I guess I haven't gotten very far down the road of being able to live with them yet." He needed to change the subject, but he didn't have a conversation starter readily at hand.

"Why did you come back here? You've lived in what I'd dare say are more interesting places."

"Sometimes things just happen. I lived in Pittsburgh well after high school and trained to be a firefighter out there. But things didn't go so well with the team of guys I was assigned to. Firefighters can be a pretty closed lot, and I wasn't one of those guys who was going to hide who I was. I told my dad I was gay when I was seventeen, and after that I got into a few fights, and then I was either accepted or left alone. The men at the station were a pretty Neanderthal lot. Most had worked there for over ten years. They did things the way they had done them for a long time, and they resented me coming in with new ideas. Mostly, once they found out I was gay, they decided they were going to run me out."

"Since you're here, it must have worked to some degree," Richard observed as he watched Morgan work, admiring his backside in those tight jeans. A familiar stirring in his lap told him he wasn't completely dead down there, but he had no intention of actually doing anything about it. After all, what would someone as hale and healthy as Morgan want with half a man like him?

"I didn't back down for a minute. I was determined to show them I was the best firefighter there was." Morgan checked the rice and began frying up the meat and vegetables, the sear and steam fragrancing the kitchen. "I'd been there about three months when there was a fire in one of the old warehouse buildings that was being turned into riverfront condos. Some of them had been sold, and a fire broke out on the top floor. We were called, and I got my gear on and raced into the building to try to get the people out. I rescued three families and escorted them out of the building while the captains were still deciding what they were going to do. The press and the mayor descended on the firehouse after that, praising me and the entire company. I never said a word, and the grumbling stopped. They also started to listen to me."

"How long did you stay after that?" The food smelled wonderful, and Richard's appetite kicked in in a huge way.

"A year. Then I got the chance to come here, and I took it. Living is more affordable here, and I had a good reputation, so I was able to command a decent salary. Because of the capitol, Harrisburg has the fire department of a larger city simply because we have to train to deal with potential fires at the large state buildings. And the state pays for that protection, so they expect very skilled, professional firefighters."

"I suppose they would." He wondered what else he could do to help prepare the meal, but Morgan seemed to have everything they way he wanted it and worked well on his own. Mostly Richard stayed out of the way, and soon Morgan was filling plates, setting them on the table.

"Would you like a beer with dinner?" Morgan asked. "I also have soda or juice if you want it."

"A beer would be nice." He reminded himself he would have only one. No more than that. It was easy for him to get carried away and decide he could bury his memories in alcohol. He had done that plenty of times, but of course it never worked for long. The alcohol only made it worse and brought out his anger and depression. "Is there anything I can do?"

"It's almost ready." Morgan set bowls on the table. "Why don't you dish up while I get the dressing?"

Richard filled the bowls, and then they sat at the table. Morgan lifted his bottle, and they clinked them before tucking in to eat. They didn't talk a great deal, and that was fine. The silences were companionable as opposed to tense, and Richard ate better than he had in a long time.

Morgan's phone rang as they were finishing, and he left the room to take it. Richard heard very little of the call, but a few times he heard Morgan say "Angus" and "You have to be kidding me." Finally Morgan wrapped up the call and returned to the kitchen. Richard resisted the urge to ask what was going on and finished the late dinner.

"The fire marshal has finished at the house, and Angus called to say that the place was hot."

"I don't know what that means."

"The fire at the house was hot, really hot, as in hotter than it ever should have been. They found traces of accelerants in the debris. They're going to want to talk to you and the family, because it looks like someone set the fire."

"Like using gasoline?"

"Or something like that, at least to start it. House fires take time to build, and they burn pretty much at a set temperature. This fire burned fast and hot, so it needed something to get it started."

"So someone set the house on fire?" Richard asked, unable to believe it. "Why?"

"That's what Angus is going to try to find out. The unusual thing is that it initially seemed like the fire started in the back of the house near the kitchen, but it started outside, in a crook of the house. Someone may have soaked the area as well as the trash cans and then lit the fire and walked away. It would have burned through the outside wall and the roof quickly if it was really hot, and once it got inside, there would be no stopping it."

"God. That means that...." Richard tried to think of why anyone would want to kill Billy's family, and then he stared at Morgan as he realized that he may have been the target of whoever did this. "My God, someone is as cold and deadly...."

"The family got out and were outside when we arrived. You were the one who was still inside." Morgan placed his fork on his empty plate and drank the last of his beer. "Why did you ask me about gasoline?"

"I don't know, other than I might remember smelling it. My memory is fuzzy and mixed up with the battlefield memories that the whole incident invoked. But the more I think about it, the more I think I smelled gasoline at some point. It was the middle of the night, but I remember my nose and throat burning, and not just from the smoke. But it's hard to really remember." He hoped it helped.

"Okay. I'll pass that on to Angus so he can look into it."

Richard nodded. "But that still means someone set the house on fire, and they wanted some of us dead." If he turned out to be the source of misery for Grace and her family, he'd never be able to forgive himself. This was a nightmare.

"Angus needs to continue investigating. I'm going to call him back. But he's going to have to involve the police, so you can expect a visit, and so can Grace and her family. Someone might have seen or heard something."

"This is going to put them through hell. They've already lost everything they have…." He pushed back from the table. "I should try to call them, though I don't know if any of their phones made it through the fire." He felt frantic.

"You can use my phone if you want," Morgan offered and handed it to him. "Make any calls you want. It's perfectly fine. You need to let people know that you're okay. Anyone local will have seen the fire on the news."

"It's just them now. I came back here because it was home, but it really hasn't felt much like it. I thought things would feel familiar, but I was gone for too long, and everyone I knew, or most everyone, has moved on." He thanked Morgan for the use of the phone and glided into the other room. "I'm sorry for being such a downer. Hopefully I'll snap out of the depressive state I've been in for the last few years and be fit company. But don't hold your breath."

Morgan grinned and threw a dish towel at him. Richard caught it and gaped at him.

"It's good to see some of your sense of humor come through. It has to mean things aren't as bad as you seem to want to make them."

"No home, everything gone, no job, and still in a chair. Yeah, the world is looking a hell of a lot brighter."

"Asshole," Morgan shot at him. "Hey, if you think I'm cutting you slack just because you're in a chair, you're crazy."

He turned away, and Richard chucked the towel back at him, smacking Morgan square in the back.

"Go make your calls."

"How long are you home? I assume you'll go back to work at some point."

"Four days. I work a three or four day on and then three or four days off. The shifts are long, so I work a lot of hours regardless, but at least I get longer time off."

"So Angus called you on your day off?" Richard asked. *no answer*

He tried to recall Grace's phone number. His own phone was gone, and of course it had all his numbers saved in it. In the end he looked it up on the Internet, but the call didn't go through. Richard tried again and found a new number, so he dialed it.

"Grace?" he asked when the call was answered. "It's Richard."

"Oh, sweetheart, are you okay? I called the hospital, and they said you'd been discharged, and I wasn't sure where you went."

She sounded frantic, and Richard felt bad for worrying her.

"The fireman who rescued me turned out to be an old friend, and he met me at the hospital and gave me a place to stay for a few days until I can figure things out. How are you? Do you all have somewhere to stay?"

"Yes. The house was insured, and they've already been by and have put us up in a hotel. They're working with the fire department to figure out what happened. They gave us some initial money to get some clothes and basic things. So we'll be okay for now. Living in a hotel isn't much fun, but they said they'll help us find temporary housing for a period of time."

She spoke so fast Richard was having trouble keeping up.

"That's good. Say hi to the kids for me, and make sure they are being taken care of. I'm okay for now. I still have to figure out what I'm going to do." He knew he should have had renter's insurance but didn't, so his things were a total loss. Not that there had been all that much. But some of what he'd lost had been irreplaceable. There had been pictures of his mom and dad that were gone forever no matter what he did.

"I will."

Richard knew she had her hands full and that she shouldn't be worrying about him. "Good. Tell them I'll try to stop by and see them in a few days once things get a little more settled." Maybe he could go shopping and get something for them.

"Don't be a stranger. I want to make sure you're really okay and not living on a park bench."

Richard was about to say he wasn't that desperate, but Grace cut him off, and she was right. He'd do what he had to, and if that meant surviving in a park, he would. He'd done worse.

"I promise. I'll call you soon. Take care, and let me know if you need anything. I'll do what I can to help." They disconnected, and he stared at the phone, trying to think of anyone else to call, and came up with nothing. He was very much alone.

"Everything okay?" Morgan asked as he walked over, carrying a laptop. "I wasn't sure if you were up for it, but I wanted to give you this. It's the laptop I told you about, and you can set it up the way you like." He placed it on the coffee table. "The Wi-Fi password is fireman234. That will get you Internet access, and from there you should be able to do what you need to."

"Thank you." He felt that was so inadequate for what Morgan was doing for him. Words didn't seem like enough. Morgan seemed like a white knight, propping him up at this stressful, unsure time.

They watched television while Richard worked a little, and then Morgan helped him down the hall into the bedroom.

"The bath is right there. Do you want to make sure you can get in and out before I go to bed?"

Morgan opened the door, and Richard maneuvered his chair inside. It was a bit of a tight fit, but he could get in and out without banging and scraping the cabinets or doorway.

"This is pretty awesome. Most places don't have doors this wide unless they're built for access." He backed out of the bathroom and returned to the bedroom. The bed was a little high, and Richard took a few seconds to figure out how he was going to shift himself out of the chair and upward. Once he had it, he relaxed a little.

"Thank you for everything," he said, not sure how he could get Morgan to leave him alone without sounding rude.

"If you need anything, let me know." Morgan squeezed his shoulder and then turned and left the room, closing the door behind him.

Now that Richard was alone, he tried to wrap his mind around Morgan and everything he'd done for him. Life had been different in the Corps, but outside it, most everyone wanted something in return for what they did. Richard kept trying to figure what Morgan could want from him, but he just kept coming back to the fact that he had nothing. Morgan seemed to be doing what he was out of kindness and old friendship. That floored him. They hadn't seen each other in almost twenty years.

"You need to let this go," he whispered to himself as he pulled one of the bags off the bed. It had the toothpaste and other things that Richard needed. He placed the bag on his lap and opened the door, then slid across the hall to the bathroom. He washed his face and hands, brushed his teeth, and used the toilet before returning to the bedroom and getting undressed.

Everything was strange to him, and by the time he was in bed, he wondered what kind of nightmares were going to visit him. They tended to get worse when he was somewhere different. At home, in his own bed where he felt safe, sometimes he could catch a break, but he had little doubt that in the strange bed and room, his mind was going to be on overdrive.

Richard levered himself up into the bed and slid in until he was under the covers. He turned off the light next to the bed and did his best to get comfortable. Then he closed his eyes and waited for sleep to come and his dreams to take over the way they had almost every single night since the incident that robbed him of so many of his brothers and left him without the use of his legs.

Chapter 3

MORGAN HALF expected to be awakened in the night by Richard's cries, but he slept soundly until his doorbell rang. "This better be good or you're in danger," Morgan growled as he yanked the door open. "Angus."

"Yeah," he said, stepping inside. "I see you didn't take time to dress. I'm sorry to disappoint you, but all this is already taken." Angus batted his eyelashes. "You know, you could get arrested."

"Shit." He looked down to where morning wood tented his briefs. Morgan hurried back to his room and grabbed a robe from his closet and shrugged it on. Then he returned to where Angus waited for him in the living room. "Sorry about that."

"How is your guest?" Angus asked as he sat on the sofa.

"He hasn't stirred yet. He had a traumatic day yesterday, and sleep is good for him." Morgan passed on what Richie had told him. "He thinks he smelled gasoline, but he isn't sure."

"It's possible. That's what we believe was used to start the fire, and those fumes can get anywhere. What's bothering us is why anyone would do that. People don't throw gasoline on the side of a stranger's house and light it on fire. It takes preparation. There must have been up to two gallons soaking the area where the fire started." Angus leaned forward. "What do you know about the guy you have staying here? It's possible he was the one they were trying to burn out."

"I knew Richie when I was a kid. He was in the Marines and lost his ability to walk. He's a good guy." Morgan knew that in his heart. Richie had been through a lot; there was no doubt about that.

"It's possible there's something in his past that's worth trying to kill for. Did you find out why he was staying there?"

"Grace's brother was one of Richie's buddies in the Marines. He grew up in the area and returned after he was discharged. His parents are gone, and it's only him. I suspect she needed a renter and he needed someplace to live. I doubt there's any huge explanation beyond that."

"All right. We've turned what we have over to the police, and they're investigating as well, but this is shooting warning bells up all over the place."

Morgan shrugged and hoped Richie wasn't the cause of this. "He's been through hell already," Morgan told Angus. "He had a family, a way of life in the Marines, that was ripped away when he wasn't able to serve any longer. Then he went through the VA system and rehab. His parents died in a car accident on their way home from visiting him. Then he moved back here and someone burns the house down where he's living? He's had enough difficulty already."

"Okay. You know we have to do this, and we're looking into the family background as well." Angus chuckled at him. "I've known you for a while, and I've never seen you this protective of anyone. What is it with this guy?"

"He's an old childhood friend."

"If you say so, but your eyes say something different. Like you want to eat him for lunch, in the best way possible. I haven't seen that look since—" Angus leaned back.

"Shut up," Morgan interrupted. "I never want to talk about that bastard again. What a loser and an asshole." Okay, so he still had anger issues when it came to Shawn. He needed to get past that.

"Yes he was, and everyone saw it but you."

"Fine. I know I have terrible taste in men. Always have."

"I don't think it's the men. You always go into each relationship as though you expect it to be temporary. You never expect them to last, and as soon as the guy shows some sort of flaw, something we all have, you back off and push him away. Shawn just did it to you first. Granted, he was a weasely asshole, but…."

"Is that what you really came for?" Morgan should have known.

"No. I was here officially, but now I'm on my break, so I thought I'd give you some shit before I had to go back to work."

Damn the man. His slight accent made even the most biting remark seem less threatening. Maybe that was why he was so good at his job. The Scottish accent got everyone talking.

"Asshole."

"Maybe. But I'm serious. When you talk about Richie, your eyes light up."

Morgan blew air through his nose. "His friendship was what I so desperately needed at a very difficult time in my life. He was also the first person I told… that I was different. It was special, and his family stood in for mine when I really needed them." He left out the part about his dad ripping all that away. The last thing he wanted was for Angus to go into character analysis mode. "Now can you leave it?" He heard Richie moving around. "I think he's up. If you want to talk to him, just go easy. I'm going to go get dressed."

"I'll be my usual gentle self."

Angus flashed a smile, and Morgan shook his head and walked down the hall, hearing Richie's door open as he closed his.

Morgan knew he probably should have told Richie about Angus, but being in the room in little more than his robe with Richie around was not a good idea. Just thinking about him got his motor running in a huge, throaty Harley kind of way, and he doubted Richie was ready for that. Hell, he wasn't ready himself. Angus was right about one thing—Morgan tended to attract weasels and losers. Morgan simply realized it at some point and ended things before they got too far down the road. Though he didn't want that with Richie… his body certainly did. He needed some distance and time to think so he could make a clearheaded decision and figure some things out.

He dressed quickly and then hurried to the bathroom. As he changed rooms, he heard Angus and Richie talking softly. Angus was a good guy, and even though they gave each other shit, Morgan knew Angus would treat Richie right. Angus was the best at what he did, and he always treated the people on the losing end of his job with care and understanding.

Once he was done, Morgan joined the two of them in the living room. "Is everything okay?" he asked Richie when he saw how pale he was. Morgan flashed Angus a hard look and turned back to Richie.

"It's nothing. He told me what you did the night of the fire, but it's…. I could dismiss it last night, but I can't now." He gripped the arms of his wheelchair hard enough his knuckles turned white. "You have to find out who did this and let me know. I'll call some friends, and we'll take out the pile of shit in small, tiny pieces if we have to. Grace is a good person, and she doesn't deserve to go through the hurt that she's going to have to endure."

"Grace and her family are going to be fine. They're insured, and while the fire was arson, we don't suspect either them or you. But we're trying to figure out why someone would do this. Do you have enemies, Mr. Smalley?"

"Please. In this area I don't know very many people at all. I came back because I thought I was coming home, but there's no one here I really remember, so how can I have enemies?"

"Maybe from the Corps? Was there someone who might want to hurt you?" Angus asked.

"The people in Baghdad whose families I ruined by killing their fathers and sons. Maybe they got together and decided to get someone to burn down the house."

"Richie, he's only trying to help. He isn't attacking you," Morgan said as gently as he could. The intensity in Richie's eyes was frightening. Morgan waited, and soon some of that fire faded away. It was still there, just burning less hot.

"I know. But it kills me to think I could be the one who brought this on Grace. She was only helping me because I served with her brother. She's a kind person."

"We aren't sure who they were after or what the motive is. We're only looking for one arsonist at this point."

"Are you working with the police?" Richie asked.

"Yes. I'm partnered with an officer for this investigation. He's meeting with Mrs. Thompson and her family now. Because I know Morgan, I agreed to speak with you."

Morgan was pleased at how Angus kept his cool and calmed Richie down with only his voice.

"I want to get to the bottom of this as badly as you do."

"I wish I could help. I honestly do." Richie said, and Morgan knew deep down that he was lying.

There was real fear and recognition in his eyes. Richie may not have been deceiving them directly, but Morgan knew in his heart that Richie wasn't being completely honest either. Whether he was able to speak about it was another story. Richie had been a Marine, and maybe he'd been out on a classified mission when everything went wrong. He wanted to give Richie the benefit of the doubt, but he was having trouble. Lies in themselves were rarely good and seldom led to anything positive.

"All right. But please either let Morgan know or give me a call if you think of anything."

Angus stood, and Morgan couldn't tell if he believed Richie or not.

"I'll let you know if I find out anything else. Morgan, I'm sure I'll be seeing you soon."

Morgan saw Angus out and closed the door. He considered what to do. "You lied," he challenged.

"No I didn't," Richie said.

"Then you didn't tell him everything, and that's the same thing."

"No, it's not. There are things I can't talk about, and as much as I want to help him and Grace, I can't." Richie pounded the arm of the wheelchair. "Do you think I like this? There is nothing I can do. I can't tell him, and I can't tell you. I don't know if it would help anyway, so give me a break."

"But you know who could do this?" Morgan said.

"I know someone who might want to harm me. That's all, but like I said, I can say no more, so please don't ask." Richie wheeled his way toward the hall. "If you want me to go, I will. I don't want to put you in danger as well."

He turned and wheeled himself down the hall. Morgan stood in place wondering, and then something clicked in the back of his mind.

"Richie," he called and hurried down the hall. "You don't have to go. I'll believe you—I do believe you."

"I don't lie, Morgan. But sometimes there are things I can't talk about. I know to you that may sound like a contradiction, but it isn't. It's all I can honestly say."

"But you were discharged."

Richie looked down at his legs. "Even though I'm half a man, I'm still a Marine, and I always will be."

Shit and damn. "Okay. I can agree that you'll always be a Marine, but you are not half a man." Morgan turned Richie to face him. "You are still yourself, and your legs have nothing to do with being a man, and you know it. If you're going to let not walking get to you, then the boy I knew at thirteen was more of a man than you are now." Morgan knew he was being harsh, but this "poor me" stuff had to end. "You're a Marine, for goodness sake, so man up!"

The storm on Richie's face was just this side of hurricane when he lifted his gaze. "How dare you."

"I dare because it's time you did something instead of feeling sorry for yourself. Let's trade places. If I were in your shoes and you were one of your Marine buddies… what would you say?" Morgan challenged, putting his hands on his hips. He cocked his head to one side, daring Richie to argue with him.

"I'm not whole. Can you see that? I can't walk, and half the time I can't even sleep because I think I'm fucking someplace else."

"So what? Marine or mouse?" he pushed. "You have to say which you are. Marines run toward the gunfire. I heard that once. So the gunfire is your legs and the flashbacks. Take them back, run toward them, and beat the living shit out of them. But don't let them beat you." Richie had never let anything get the better of him. Not when they were kids. "What happened to the kid who could do anything?"

"He died some time ago," Richie said.

"Then revive him. So you're in a chair. Who cares? I don't."

"How can you not?" Richie asked, more loudly than was necessary.

"That's easy. Like this." Morgan leaned forward and kissed Richie hard and deep, pushing him against the back of the chair. "Does this feel like I give a fuck if you're in the chair or not?" He kissed Richie again, even harder, taking possession of his mouth before he could answer. Morgan hoped Richie was stunned and not horrified. He got his answer when Richie's arms slipped around his neck and he returned the kiss.

By the time he pulled back once again, Morgan needed air badly, but he hadn't wanted to break the kiss, so he waited until the last possible second.

"Damn," Richie groaned.

"Yeah, that was definitely damn. Now did you learn your lesson, or do I need to do that again?" Morgan teased.

"I think I got the point, but you better try one more time just to make sure the lesson is well learned."

Morgan didn't have to be asked twice. Richie tasted earthy and rich, with a touch of sweet and a lot of heat that shot through Morgan like a bolt of lightning.

"Okay," Morgan whispered when he had to breathe again. "I think you got the point."

"So what do we do about it?"

"I'm not sure yet." Morgan needed his head to stop spinning before he could fucking think straight. All the blood had rushed south, and he needed a chance to let it equalize once again. "You need to help Angus figure out what's going on. You may not be able to tell him the whys, but you can tell him the who. Otherwise you could still be in danger." And by extension, so could Morgan. He tried not to focus on that. "I know there are secrets that can't be divulged, but you need to figure out what you can say to help us help you."

"I don't know what I can tell you."

"Then figure it out, because if this guy goes after someone else and you could have helped, you don't want that on your conscience."

"I know…," Richie said. "But I don't know what I can say. The operation and everything around it is classified."

"I'm not asking about the operation or why you feel the way you do. If you can't talk, then you can't. But if there is someone who you think might be after you…."

"That's it—I don't know. For one operation, they brought in a specialist from outside our group, and he was really good at what he did. Which I can't say, but he was also fascinated by fire, and I'm the one who got him busted and booted because of it." Richie was clearly conflicted. "Don't ask me what he did or anything else, but his name is Bradley Moser. He may not even be in this part of the country."

"Okay. Do you know anything about him? Like where he's originally from?"

"Raleigh is what he said was home, but it could have been a lie. There was a lot about him that didn't add up for any of us. We didn't trust him, and it was a good thing we didn't, because he wasn't everything he was supposed to be."

"Okay. I'll tell Angus, and he can get to work on this guy. It does seem like a long shot, but then we don't know the background. We do know he was a Marine, though."

43

Morgan pulled out his phone and called Angus. Then he let Richie and Angus talk. He didn't listen in, figuring if anything was secret, the less he knew the better at this point. Finally Richie rolled back into the living room and handed him the phone.

"I guess that's done." Richie seemed shaken. "I think that's as close as I've ever come to divulging secret information. Usually we simply don't talk about our missions. Sometimes parts or all of them are secret, so we just keep quiet. It's the safest course. Loose lips sink ships and all that."

"Well, this is to help keep you safe." Morgan walked to where Richie sat.

"What do I do now?" Richie asked.

"We wait and see what Angus can find out. He's very good at digging, and he'll have access to police resources and databases. Between him and Antonio—he's the police detective he usually works with—they're pretty unbeatable. Though Antonio can be a real ass at times."

"Are they a couple?"

"God no. If they were they'd kill each other. Angus is with Kevin."

"Oh yeah, you told me that. Sorry, I don't like it when I get forgetful. I used to be able to remember everything. Now my mind gets scattered, and I hate that. People think I'm not paying attention, but sometimes information doesn't get stored right or something."

"It's okay. Up till now, Angus was just a name." Morgan backed away. "We should eat and then figure out what we're going to do today." Morgan was trying to process everything that had already happened this morning, but the one thing that stuck with him over everything else was the kiss, or kisses. Damn, they were imprinted on his brain and would stay there for as long as he lived.

"What can I do to help?"

"Why don't you put those chef wannabe skills to use and help me with brunch? We both slept through breakfast, so I'll whip up some eggs, and I think there is fruit in the refrigerator. A lot of the guys eat out a lot, but I prefer to cook as much as I can. At the station, meals can be grab and go, so when I'm home I try to make as much fresh food as I can." It didn't always work out, but fresh stuff was always better.

They worked together in the kitchen. Richie was a huge help, and soon they'd prepared eggs, some ham, fresh fruit, and even muffins—granted, they weren't from scratch, but the scents filled the kitchen with warmth. They sat down, and both ate ravenously.

"What do you usually do on a day off?" Richie asked.

"Rest, get caught up on chores, go to the gym. I have some guys I meet in the afternoon when I'm off. They're pretty cool, and we work out together when we can. Well, they work out every day, and I join them when I can." He wasn't sure if Richie would be interested in that or not. "You could come with me if you wanted."

"What am I going to do there?"

"Arms, chest, back. I'm sure there are plenty of exercises you could do, and they have seats that will lower you into the pool and whirlpool if you want. It's fully accessible."

Richie wasn't convinced; that was obvious. "I used special equipment at the VA hospital. How am I supposed to get out of my chair and onto a weight bench and back again? It isn't easy, and it definitely isn't pretty."

"I could help you," Morgan offered.

"And how would you feel if you had to have someone pick you up and carry you to a bench and then carry you back like you were useless? Because that's how I feel. Sure, I'd love to be able to go to a gym like a normal person. Marines are trained and conditioned into top physical form, but doing that for me is a huge pain. I went to a gym once before I moved here, and everyone stared at me like I was some freak from another planet." He pushed away from the table.

"I have no intention of carrying you anywhere. You can do whatever you like, and there are plenty of things you can do perfectly well on your own. But if you don't want to try, that's up to you."

Richie huffed. "You're worse than my mother was. She pushed me while I was in the rehab facility to do more, but she could take lessons from you."

"I was raised Catholic—guilt is something I can do very well." Morgan smiled. "Well, I was Catholic as a kid. Maybe it just comes naturally."

"Well, stop it. I'll come to the gym with you this afternoon."

"Good." Morgan opened the hall closet door and dragged out the vacuum cleaner. The house didn't clean itself, and it had been a while since the place had gotten a good scrubbing, so he got to work.

The house wasn't that large, so cleaning didn't take all day. Richie helped where he could, but Morgan did the bulk of it and finished up in little more than an hour. The house smelled mostly of lemon. He preferred those cleaners over the pine-scented ones, which made him sneeze.

"Let me put all this stuff away, and we can get ready to go."

"I don't have any workout clothes," Richie said.

"I have some sweatpants and a T-shirt you can wear," Morgan said and hurried to his room. Digging around in his closet, he found an extra bag and the clothes Richie could wear.

"I feel like some poor relation," Richie said, taking the bag.

"If you like it, we can arrange to get you some workout clothes of your own." Morgan knew just the place, of course. "You're only borrowing them." He understood pride and making your own way. He'd made his own path, and losing everything had to be a real kick in the backside. "Don't let your pride stand in your way."

Richie turned toward the window. "My pride is about all I have left."

"No, it's not. You have plenty left, and people who care about you. Stop being so defeatist. You're Richie, and you can do whatever you want as long as you're willing to get up off your keister and do it."

Richie looked him up and down.

"What?"

"I was looking for a set of pom-poms and a cheerleading outfit."

Morgan placed both hands on the handles of Richie's wheelchair. "Sometimes we all need a cheerleader. Your mother was one of the best. She encouraged both of us all the time."

"I know. She'd be the first to kick me in the ass right about now."

"So get your bag packed, and we'll head on over to the gym. The guys will be getting there soon, and I'd really like you to meet them. They're a hoot." Morgan left to get his own bag packed. In less than ten minutes, they were both ready and in the car, on their way to the gym. To Morgan it felt like a victory of some sort.

THE GUYS had been great, declaring that they were working arms and including Richie in their routine. They'd figured out ways to work around any impediment, and Richie seemed to have a great time. Until the workout was over and everyone headed to the locker room.

"What is it?"

"Changing clothes isn't a pretty sight."

"You don't have to be elegant. It's a locker room. Believe me, Howard can barely put his pants on without falling over."

"It isn't that." Richie looked up at him plaintively. "My legs. They're not pretty. They were injured, and I have a lot of scars that start there and go up to my back. They said they were lucky to save my legs at all. Of course, that was when they were hopeful that I'd be able to walk again, but that hasn't proved to be the case."

"What do you want to do? We can go home, but then you can't use the pool and whirlpool, which might do you good." It was up to Richie, and he'd do what he wanted.

"No. It's okay." Richie raised his gaze straight ahead. "I have to stop hiding, and that means all of it."

He rolled to the locker room, and Morgan followed. Inside, he got Richie set up with a locker and a place with enough space for his chair. Richie did keep the back of his chair to most of the locker area, but once he'd stripped down, Morgan got a look at his legs. They were thin in proportion to the rest of him, with long scars along his hips and knees. There were smaller ones as well, probably the injuries themselves as opposed to surgical scars.

"Not pretty, is it?" Richie said as he pulled up his leg to put on the bathing trunks Morgan had found for him.

"They're your legs," he said. "They look how they look." He didn't see anything wrong. "Those are battle wounds."

"So…?"

Morgan leaned close. "Battle wounds are sexy," he whispered.

Richie stared at him in disbelief. "Is that some sort of kinky thing? It's scars and twisted legs that do it for you?"

"No. You're a warrior, and you have the scars to prove it." Morgan pulled up his shirtsleeve. "I got this from rescuing a three-year-old from his bedroom." Morgan took off his shirt and then dropped his pants so he could get into his bathing suit. "The cut on my leg is from falling through a floor to the basement. I managed not to break anything and got out with just the cut. If you want more, I have tons of them all over me. It's part of what I do every day, and I'd do each and every one of them again." Morgan pulled up his suit after forgetting himself and flashing his ass at Richie. "I bet each of your scars has a story too, so don't be ashamed of them."

Every time he turned around, he ran into another area of insecurity, which made Morgan wonder what had happened to Richie. The confident kid he'd known was a long time ago, but Marines had to have confidence and strength. It seemed those qualities had been yanked out of Richie, and he wished he could find them and put them back.

"Let's go swim." He grabbed the towels and slid his feet into shower shoes before leading Richie back through the shower area. "That one is fully accessible, with a seat and everything."

"Thanks," Richie said and kept going through.

The pool area was large, with a huge wall of windows. Richie asked to swim, so Morgan held the chair while Richie shifted to the swim seat and pressed the button to lower it. As soon as he could, Richie slipped off the chair into the water and became someone else. He took off, cutting through the water. Morgan put the chair against the wall and got in as well. He wasn't much of a swimmer, using the water to relax, but Richie got in one of the lanes and began swimming laps. The usual swimmers stopped what they were doing, watching him cut through the water at a brisk pace.

"Go, man," one of them said, watching one of the timing clocks. "Geez, he's really booking." They got into the water and began swimming along with Richie.

"I guess the water was good for him," Morgan's friend Tristan said as he stood next to him.

"He's really self-conscious about so many things," Morgan said without taking his gaze off Richie. He has no reason to be."

"Nope. But injuries, especially bad ones, can alter your self-image. Instead of the healthy and hale person you were, now there's pain, limitations, and things you want to do but can't." Tristan smacked him lightly on the back. "You remember the last time you got burned or something? You couldn't do a lot of things, no sauna or whirlpool, and using your arms hurt like hell for weeks. You were a full-on pain in the ass, and that was temporary until you healed. His is permanent." Tristan walked toward the whirlpool. "Come on. Let's bubble a little while. At least you can stop drooling over him for a few minutes."

"I'm not drooling," Morgan protested and followed Tristan back.

Tristan stepped down into the otherwise empty whirlpool. "You've been eye-fucking him ever since he put on that T-shirt that was tight in all the right places."

Tristan leaned back, and Morgan got in as well. Tristan's partner, Brent, joined them right after.

"I have not."

"What are you two arguing about?" Brent settled next to Tristan, close enough that they were probably holding hands under the water.

"Morgan's eye-fucking Richie," Tristan said.

"You so were," Brent said. "Not that he wasn't doing it in return. Every time you did a set, he watched you like a hawk. Granted, half the guys in the gym were watching as well, but not the way he was."

Brent shifted so the jet was aimed where he wanted it, and Morgan looked over at the pool in case Richie needed him.

"Where did you meet this guy?"

"We were kids together, and then we met again at a fire when the place he was staying burned down."

"Did you know he was gay back then?" Tristan asked.

"Yeah. We were each the first person we told, but then I moved away."

Tristan and Brent shared one of those looks, like they were talking to each other without words. Morgan hated when they did that.

"Did you have a connection back then?" Tristan asked.

"Yeah. He was my best friend. The best I ever had. It killed me when my dad moved us away. It was like part of myself—" And there the two of them went again, eye-talking between them that no one could miss.

"What?" Morgan asked, turning to watch Richie once more. He was resting, arms hooked over the edge of the pool, a brilliant smile on his face that reminded Morgan of the kid he'd once been. The smile reached almost to his ears, and his dimples were deep and sexy.

"Nothing," Tristan said. "Do you think he's about ready to get out?"

Morgan waved, and Richie swam over. "How much longer do you want to swim?"

"About fifteen minutes," Richie said, and Morgan nodded and smiled. Richie swam off, and Morgan settled in the tub once again. It was perfect—warm without being too hot.

"So you just reconnected with him?" Tristan said.

"Yeah. Yesterday."

"He seems to be doing okay. If he were having troubles, he'd be coughing, wouldn't he?" Brent asked.

"Yeah. Maybe what he needed was to get out and be around people again."

"Maybe what he needed was a friend who really cared about him again. Things change once part of the person you were has been ripped away. He needs time to heal around people who will support him." Tristan stood and walked over to where Morgan was sitting. He leaned on the edge of the whirlpool, watching Richie. "He has determination and guts in spades."

"He always did."

"Maybe he just needs to remember that, and maybe remember who he was." Tristan turned to him. "He's the same man he always was. He needs to see himself that way."

"I know. But how do I get him to do that?"

Tristan looked to Brent, who shrugged. "Yeah. I wish I knew too. Give him some time and some care. Maybe find a way for him to feel valued again. He said he was out of the Corps, so I'm assuming they discharged him. The one thing he was good at, or thinks he was good at, has been taken away. So he needs to find something to replace it."

"How do I do that?" Morgan asked. He stood and sat on the edge to cool off.

"You can't. That's something he has to do for himself. He's probably lost a lot of his self-image and self-esteem, so he's the one who has to rebuild it. I know it sucks, but that's how it has to be."

"How do you know all this?"

"I've been working toward my degree in psychology, so I've been studying situations like this. I was hoping to work with veterans and people with PTSD, like what Richie may be experiencing." Tristan turned back to the pool. "I think he's about done."

Morgan nodded and stood, getting out of the whirlpool and slipping on his shower shoes before walking to the lift chair. He pressed the button to lower it into the pool, and Richie sat on it. Then Morgan raised the chair, water running off it and Richie as it lifted him out of the water. Morgan brought the chair over, and Richie shifted over to it. "I have your towel." Morgan handed it to Richie and pushed him to the shower area.

Morgan got Richie to the accessible shower and then left him alone. He wasn't sure how much help would be welcome, and Richie had been taking care of himself for a while without him, so he thought Richie would be okay. He did take the shower next to it and listened closely as he stripped off his suit and stepped under the spray, pulling the curtain closed. It wasn't long before he heard the water in Richie's stall and took that as a good sign.

He showered carefully and quickly, then turned off the water and grabbed his towel, drying off and wrapping it around his waist before stepping out. Richie was still in the stall, so he stayed close, trying not to look like he was concerned. He heard the water turn off, and a few minutes later, Richie pulled his chair close and then pushed aside the curtain and shifted to his chair.

"You didn't have to wait," Richie said.

"I wasn't," Morgan protested and headed for the door. He held it for Richie and did his best not to watch him too closely. Richie was every bit what he'd expected of a Marine, a strong upper body, lean, with banked power that seemed to strain to be let out.

Morgan carried his wet suit back to his locker and began the process of getting dressed. Richie was close, doing the same. In fact, Morgan was aware of Richie the entire time, like he had some radar that was tuned to him and only him. "Are you about ready?" Morgan asked once he sat down to put on his shoes.

"Just a few minutes."

"Do you want to have dinner? The guys go out after workouts, and we're welcome to go with them if you want. I sometimes do, and it's a good time."

"They don't really know me," Richie said.

"They will if you want them to." Morgan put all his wet stuff in the special pocket in his bag and gathered it together. Richie was still getting dressed, so Morgan sat on the bench to wait.

"Then let's go to dinner," Richie said.

Morgan went to tell the guys. They were gathering out front, and he let them know that Richie and he were coming. Then he returned to the locker room and saw Richie putting his wallet back in his pocket. God, Richie must have been worried if he could afford to go out to dinner. Morgan kept that bit of information to himself and grabbed his bag while Richie placed his on his lap, and they left the locker room.

"That really felt great," Richie said as they moved. "I used to love to swim, and I did a lot of it for therapy. I guess I was better than I thought."

"You were amazing. How do you go so fast without using your legs? I mean, that's where a lot of the power is."

"Moving my legs is problematic, and I can keep my legs together, and then I flex my hips to make my legs go up and down to displace the water and help me move forward. It helps strengthen the muscles I'm not able to use."

They reached the front door.

"Where are we going?" Morgan asked.

"There's a great steak place that just opened on the pike. We can go there," Tristan offered, and they all agreed and started heading out to their cars.

"I'll call ahead," Tristan said.

Morgan waved, and he and Richie headed to his car.

"They seem so nice."

"They all are. Tristan is a student and had done some modeling, mostly for Brent. It's how they met. Brent's a photographer, and he's becoming very well known. They've been together a few years. The other guys are straight but supportive. We all tease each other, and most of the others can't seem to find a girl that will put up with them for more than a few months." He unlocked the car and opened the passenger door. "I was starting to wonder if they really were straight, but now I think they're just too wrapped up in themselves and their own lives and priorities."

"Sounds like a pretty self-centered bunch to me," Richie said before pulling the door closed.

Morgan placed the chair on the floor of the backseat and then got in. "They're young and are still figuring out what they want. Cars and careers are more important than steady girls right now. They have some money and spend their free time working out and trying to get what they want from the girls in clubs and bars. That'll all change soon enough. Mike met this girl a few months ago, and he's been dating her ever since. I think it could be serious, and once he gets serious, the rest will probably follow."

He pulled out of the lot and drove the few miles to the restaurant, noticing that Richie watched out the windows the entire time, scanning the area like they were in a combat zone. He hadn't noticed it on the way over, but it was very evident now. Richie was guitar-string tense and winding tighter by the second. "Richie, what's wrong?"

"Nothing," he answered defensively.

"This isn't a battlefield," Morgan commented as gently as he could. He didn't want to put Richie further on edge.

"Sorry." Richie relaxed some into the seat. "I do that sometimes without thinking. I've been so conditioned to be aware of everything around me that I go into recon mode without thinking about it."

He was breathing heavily, but Morgan said nothing as he continued the drive to the restaurant.

"The man two cars ahead has probably had too much to drink, so you might want to…."

Before Richie could finish what he was saying, the car in question veered into the next lane, causing that driver to swerve and then try to move back, but he overcompensated and slid into the next lane. Morgan slowed and pressed the brakes, checking his mirror before hitting them harder yet. He managed to change lanes and narrowly avoided being clipped by the car in front of him, which was now also out of control after being hit. The sound of metal rang in the car, and it took Morgan a second to realize that it was coming from outside and that they were past the accident. He slowed and pulled off the road. He already had his phone out before he opened the door and his feet hit the ground.

"911 Emergency."

"This is Morgan Ayers, Harrisburg Fire Department. I just witnessed an automobile accident on Carlisle Pike near Best Buy. Please dispatch police, fire, and ambulances. One of the drivers was driving erratically, and alcohol may be involved. I'm going to assist." He answered the operator's questions as he got closer.

"Emergency services have been dispatched."

"Thank you." Morgan hung up and approached the car that had been hit. The back of the car was intact, but the front had been severely damaged. He got the back door open, and two young children stared at him with terror in their eyes. "Is everyone all right?"

"I am, and the kids seem to be, but I'm not sure about my husband," a woman answered from the passenger seat.

"I'm a firefighter, and I'm going to get you out. Can you open your door?" He waited as she tried it, and the door screeched and opened about halfway.

"It won't go any farther," she said.

Then the door was wrenched open, metal screaming.

"I got it," Richie said from his chair on the grass.

Morgan was going to ask how he got out and over, but that was for a later time. He told the kids to unbuckle and get out that door.

"Don't use that one." He pointed at the driver's side, and they filed out, bursting into tears as soon as they were in their mother's arms. Now that the other door was open, Morgan leaned in across the passenger seat to the driver. He felt his neck and got a pulse, which was a huge relief. Sirens sounded in the distance, getting louder fast as they overlapped one another, police, ambulances, and fire rescue all converging.

Morgan backed out of the car and met the police officer. "I made the phone call. I'm a Harrisburg firefighter. The driver of the light blue Corolla was weaving. You'll want to have someone check his breath. I've got three people out of this vehicle. One is still inside. He's alive and needs help."

"Thanks," the officer said as emergency personnel descended on the vehicle.

Morgan told the EMTs what he knew and then got out of the way. The rescue teams got the car door open and began working on the driver.

"He's alive," Morgan told the woman from the car. At least he had been a few minutes earlier, but Morgan kept that to himself.

They got him out of the car and onto a stretcher.

"Lily," a rough voice groaned, and she hurried over to him. "I'm going to be okay."

She was crying and so were the children, but it appeared that tragedy had been averted. He found Richie with the youngest child sitting on his lap in the chair, holding him as she watched her mother.

"This is Macy," Richie said gently. "She climbed up here when her mother's arms were full of her little brother."

Lily stepped back from the stretcher and returned to where they were waiting. Macy climbed down and hurried over to her as she got closer.

"Thank you both for your help. He's talking, and they've bandaged his arm and leg. The police will want to talk to me, I'm sure."

"Us too," Morgan said, and on cue, the officer he'd spoken with earlier approached.

He took the woman aside and spoke with her for a few minutes, then approached Morgan and Richie. "Did you both see what happened?"

"Yes," Richie answered and went into a detailed account of what he'd seen and why he thought the driver might have been under the influence. The officer wrote frantically as Richie talked. By the time he was done, all Morgan could add was that he agreed with Richie. His account had to be an officer's dream. "I was in the service and am trained to observe."

"Very good." He took both their names. "If we have any more questions I'll be in contact, but it seems we have all we need. You're free to go."

"Thanks," Richie answered and began wheeling himself back to the car. Morgan watched him go and wondered where this particular in-charge, confident Richie had suddenly come from. It was attractive—hell, it was hot. Morgan shook his head as he followed him back to the car after texting the guys that they were delayed and were now on their way.

The guys were all seated and had their drinks by the time they arrived.

"We waited for you."

"There was an accident, and Morgan stopped to help," Richie said, rolling up to the chairless place that had been left for him. "It was a mess. Some guy was likely drunk already and collided with a family car with children in the backseat."

"The kids were fine, shaken up but not injured. Their father was hurt and was being taken to the hospital." Morgan took the place across from Richie. "Have you all ordered?" He looked over the menu, quickly deciding what he wanted. They apparently hadn't placed their orders but were about to. He set his menu aside.

Richie sat staring blankly at him, the menu open, but he didn't seem to be paying attention to it.

"Do you know what you want?" Morgan asked, but Richie didn't answer. He reached over, touching his hand. "Have you decided?"

Richie picked up the menu. Morgan was concerned, but none of the others seemed to have picked up on it. Their conversation continued, with Brent telling stories about sittings and what some clients asked for.

"I had a woman ask for boudoir photos for her husband when she made the appointment, and then the two of them showed up, and they decided they wanted me to take pictures of them… more active… shall we say." The guys laughed, and Richie did the same, but it didn't seem genuine.

Morgan had a flash of insight. "Is it your parents?" he asked, and Richie nodded. "Sorry."

"They weren't as lucky as the family today."

"No. These people were very lucky. They had a good car, and it could have been worse. But I'm worried about you."

"I'll be fine." Richie steadied himself like he was trying to force away what he couldn't stop. The server approached the table and took their orders.

"I bet you have some interesting stories," Mike said from the far side of the table, leaning forward so he could see to their end.

"Yeah. But most of them aren't dinner conversation," Richie said.

"What was it like in Iraq?" Mike asked. "I mean, we saw stuff on the news."

"It was hot, and most of the time sand got everywhere you didn't want it, especially when it was windy. It didn't matter where you were or what you did, sand got everywhere…." Richie squirmed slightly. "And I mean everywhere. It was so dry your skin would crack sometimes, and the sun felt like you were in a broiler, and there was no escaping it. Shade helped some, but not much when it was over one hundred degrees. All you could do was drink water like crazy because you sweated through everything, and the more you sweated, the more the sand stuck to you."

"Was basic training hard?" Tristan asked.

"It was brutal and designed to test everything about you from the ground up and the inside out. I was young when I joined up and had all the confidence of youth, so of course I thought I could do anything. I did well, but I learned that there were limits, and they were tested each and every day."

"So did you like it?" Brent asked.

"Yeah. The guys were like a family. We'd all been through the same trials and had come out the other end. That's part of the training as well. You come to rely on your brothers because you can't do it all."

The server brought their drinks, and Morgan picked his up absently, drawn into Richie's story the way the others were.

"You also learned to watch each other's back, because contrary to what we all thought about our mothers, no one has eyes in the back of their head, so one of your brothers was always watching the other way. That's how we survived." He drank half his water and set the mug on the table.

"Do you miss it?" Joseph, one of the other guys asked. Joseph was huge, and to look at him, you'd think he was a muscle-bound ape, but he was one of the smartest men Morgan knew and was currently working on a master's in biology.

"Yeah, I do. They were like part of my family. I knew the guys in my unit the way you know your brothers or cousins. We ate, slept, did everything together."

"It's okay. It's hard for those of us who haven't experienced it to understand."

Richie nodded. "During my second year, we were in the north working with some of the groups in the mountains, and it was cold as hell. The patrol bunked down in what had once been a nice house but was now just a shell. It was shelter but cold. We slept on a concrete floor, curled next to each other like puppies to share warmth. It was survival, and none of us thought twice about it. It was what we had to do to make sure we were all safe and made it through the night."

The food began to arrive, and the conversation drifted to other topics. Morgan figured the guys were still curious, but they were guys, and when food was involved, that pretty much became the center of the universe for a short period of time. He ate his steak but also ended up watching Richie, who ate some and then picked at what was left. "Is it okay?" Morgan asked.

Richie nodded and went back to eating.

"You know, you were a huge help at the scene of the accident. How did you get out of the car?"

"Your car is a two door, and you put the chair behind my seat. I pulled it out and got into it. I guess I was lucky it's been dry, because if it had been muddy I'd have had trouble rolling on the grass. Once I was out, I figured you could use a hand."

"I needed one. Those kids were really shaken up, and their mother was just as bad. Sometimes another set of hands is really nice, and that little girl seemed taken with you."

"It's the chair. Half the time people only see the chair, and other times they think because I'm in a chair I'm harmless and useless. Children seem to see past that and are actually interested in me. She asked about my chair as I was holding her and said it was 'sweet' that I always had my own chair."

Morgan couldn't stop the laughter. "Children are honest."

Richie bit his lower lip, a move that Morgan was coming to understand represented Richie's nervousness.

"Do you see me or the chair?"

At least Richie was being straightforward.

"I see my oldest friend, now an attractive man. That you're in a chair is relatively immaterial. I mean, I know you are, and that has implications for your life, but in a material way, it doesn't matter. It's like you come with more hardware than most people."

"That's a good way to put it," Tristan chimed in.

"It's just honest."

Morgan answered Tristan, but he looked at Richie. He wanted him to understand, and Richie's eyes brightened. He seemed to have received the answer he was looking for. Richie returned to his dinner with what looked like a renewed appetite, and Morgan did the same.

"When do you go back on shift?" Mike asked him.

"Tuesday morning. I'm on for four days and then off for three once again. Four days of twelve-hour shifts and then three days off."

"It seems like too many hours," Brent said.

"It does, but it has to do with mealtimes, breaks, and the fact that there is a lot of downtime. It works out in the end, and I have enough time off that I can really rest and get things done around the house." He finished his dinner and sat back while the conversation moved away from him. He was happiest that way. When the topic turned to the latest video games, he tuned back in.

"They've added a game to our training," Morgan interjected. "The partner of one of the firefighters is a designer, and he developed a fire training game that contains buildings specific to our area, including the capitol. It's pretty awesome, and the graphics are impressive."

"That sounds awesome. Can anyone play, or do you have to be a firefighter?" Richie asked.

"It's exclusive to the department, and it's geared to very specific firefighting procedures and protocols. It's a big enough hit that other departments are making requests. You haven't met Kevin—he's Angus's partner. The two of them worked together to develop and perfect it, and I got to have some input as well." He leaned closer to Richie. "He even gave me a consulting credit on the game. That was so nice of him."

"I'd like to see it. We used to play a lot of games on deployment. Mostly war games, of course." Richie thanked the server when she took his plate and asked for a cup of coffee. "During downtime we used to have tournaments of all kinds. The military is hurry up and wait, and we did plenty of waiting and needed something to pass the time. They'd tell us to be ready to go, which meant we had to stay on base, close to our barracks, for sometimes weeks at a time, so computer time and video games were a huge entertainment."

"How about I see if I can bring you to the station so you can see the game? I'm not allowed to bring it home because it's proprietary."

"That would be cool," Richie said delightedly.

It was nice to see him excited about something. Morgan wondered if he should get a video game console if Richie got that excited about them.

The party began to break up a few minutes later as the server brought the checks. Morgan paid for their dinners, taking Richie's check when he wasn't looking. Then they said good-bye and exited the restaurant.

The night was a little cool but hinted that warmer weather was on its way. "I love this time of year. Summer is just around the corner, and we can sit out in the backyard and relax in the evening summer air."

"I put up with winter in order to get through to summer."

"Exactly. This is the start of the best time of year to be outside. Of course, it's also one of the busiest times of year at work. When it gets hot and dry, people lose control of grills and tax old electrical systems with air conditioners. The only busier time is the holidays, when everyone overloads their house with Christmas lights. Of course, in summer there are also a lot of emergency calls because of the heat."

"Geez," Richie said, smacking him lightly on the arm. "You really have a way of adding to the fun and excitement, don't you?"

"Are you teasing me?" Morgan asked as they headed to the car.

"Of course I am. You were talking about how you love this time of year and began waxing poetic about how people set things on fire. You know nothing says summer like a discussion on fire safety."

"Okay. I get the point." He raised his hands in submission.

"Good." Richie pulled open the door and slid into the seat. Morgan folded up his chair and slid it behind him. "I mean, if you're standing outside on a nice spring evening, there are much better topics you could bring up if you were... say... trying to impress someone or...."

"Okay. How about, we didn't get dessert, so we could stop for ice cream on the way home? There's a great place that makes their own a few blocks from the house."

"That would be nice."

Richie grinned at him, and enough heat raced through him that he knew no amount of ice cream was going to cool him down.

Chapter 4

TENSION FILLED him, but it was different than the type that went with his PTSD. This was good, and it was only between him and Morgan. Richard sat in the passenger seat, his hand itching to touch, but he kept it in his lap. Morgan had been nice, and he'd said the right things, but that still didn't mean he was truly interested in him... like that. Morgan had kissed him, but that was to make a point. He didn't know if the kisses had stolen Morgan's breath the way they'd ripped it from Richard's chest and left him empty and gasping when they ended.

And seeing Morgan in action, calm and capable, knowing what to do and how to help. He took charge and got those kids out. He even helped the injured man until the ambulance arrived. Morgan was amazing, and he was sitting right next to him, but Richard was too damned afraid to do anything about it. Morgan was right. He had lost some part of himself. He used to be confident and self-assured. Now he was acting like a teenage girl on her way home from a first date, wondering if he really liked her or not. He was so pathetic.

"Can we go right home?" Richard asked as they approached the area. He wasn't in the mood for ice cream. What he needed was to go to his room, be alone, and spend some time licking his wounds and trying to figure out what he was going to do with the rest of his life. He certainly couldn't go on like this.

"If that's what you'd like," Morgan said and made the turn to his house. "Not have a taste for rocky road?"

God, Morgan had remembered his favorite. "Maybe some other time."

When Morgan touched his leg, he jumped. It was sharp, and while not painful, more sensation than he'd become used to having. Since his injury, sensation in his legs had been muted, like someone was touching him long distance. But this was immediate and deep.

"Did I hurt you?" Morgan asked.

"No." Richard calmed down. He'd had things like this happen before. His brain played tricks on him sometimes. Sensory disturbance they called it. At one point, he hadn't been able to move his legs, but it had felt like someone was bending them toward his head. The pain and the weirdness were overwhelming, especially when he could see his legs lying still. "Just some weird sensations. I get them every once in a while." Morgan had pulled his hand away, and Richard wished he'd put it back. "It's usually temporary."

Morgan kept his hands on the wheel for the rest of the ride to his house. Richard was able to get himself out of the car, once Morgan retrieved his chair and the door closed, but Morgan helped him with the steps.

Inside, everything seemed small and close, and the whole house smelled like Morgan. He went to get a drink of water, and after filling the glass, he turned his chair around and nearly ran over Morgan's feet. He finished the water and placed the glass on the counter. "I think I'm going to go to bed. I did a lot today and should probably rest." He needed to get to his room. "Thank you for everything."

He wheeled out of the room and refused to look back at Morgan. The glimpse he did get was of stunned surprise, but he needed to think, and he couldn't do that with Morgan's hot firemanness nearby all the time.

"All right. Good night," Morgan said.

Something in his voice made Richard stop at the hallway. "Good night," he said, not daring to turn to look. He continued down the hallway to the bedroom and went inside, where he got his things to clean up.

He worked quickly, brushing his teeth and washing up before returning to the bedroom. He got undressed and into bed. He didn't relax for a second. Richard lay between the cool sheets, listening as Morgan moved through the house and then down the hallway. Richard thought he may have stopped outside. He imagined him outside the door but then heard no more footsteps, and the light from under the door went dark. Finally he relaxed and rolled over, telling errant parts of his body not to get their hopes up or anything. It didn't matter what he or his dick wanted. Morgan was better off without being burdened with a guy like him. He was a man of action, and no matter what he said, Morgan didn't need to be weighed down by a guy who couldn't walk.

"Richie."

He rolled over, seeing the door partially open. "I'm awake."

Morgan stepped into the room, leaving the door open. "What's going on with you?"

"I don't know what you mean." Richard swallowed.

Morgan came closer, his wide-shouldered form outlined by the dim light from the bathroom across the hall. "Yes you do. I see what's in your eyes most of the time, and then you pull away. Is this some kind of game?"

"I don't play those games." Richard used his arms to lever himself up. "I…."

"If you don't play games, then what's with the hot and cold?" Morgan stood still about halfway between him and the doorway.

"You deserve better, okay? I have nothing, and there isn't the brightest of futures ahead for me. I'll always be in the chair, and I can't do what I love, and… you deserve a whole person."

"You'd be more man than most of the people I know if you were missing your legs and both arms." Morgan came closer. "Don't you understand? What makes you a man isn't on the outside. It's what's in here," Morgan said, touching Richard's bare chest. "The question is, are you brave enough to let me see it?"

Morgan leaned over the bed, and Richie hoped he got even closer.

Their lips touched, and Richie surged forward, kissing Morgan hard. He'd been too cowardly earlier to say what he wanted, but now that it had come to pass anyway, he latched on and took it, pulling Morgan down. When Morgan's bare chest touched his, everything felt right.

"Are you sure this is what you want?" Morgan asked. "I've thought about you and dreamed of you off and on since we were kids." Morgan was shaking as he spoke. "This is too good to be true."

Richard didn't know what to say to that. "We're friends. This will change that."

"I know," Morgan said and kissed him again.

Richard's head spun. He wanted more and wrapped his arms around Morgan. Hard muscle under warm, smooth skin slid beneath his hands. Morgan was hard wherever he touched, and damn if that wasn't a turn-on. Morgan pressed him down onto the bed once again.

"I need to shift."

"Sweetheart," Morgan began, standing next to the bed. "You get yourself comfortable."

He pushed the last of his clothes down his legs. Richard watched unmoving until Morgan stood naked next to his bed. He couldn't tear his eyes away. Morgan was a thing of powerful, masculine beauty. Richard had gotten a few furtive glimpses at the gym, but here he stood, legs apart, hands on his hips, letting Richard look his fill.

Finally he was able to move, and lay back down, pillow under his head. Morgan crawled onto the bed, moving slowly, straddling him. "You have to promise you'll tell me if I hurt you." Morgan's gaze met his firmly. "You must promise."

"I will," Richard agreed, but he knew deep down Morgan wouldn't cause him pain. "I'm not made of glass either."

"I know that." He kissed him again, brought their bodies together.

Even though he couldn't move his legs, he knew Morgan had a way with his body. Morgan knew how to touch him, firmly yet gently. There was care and yet enough sensation that Richard pressed upward when Morgan stroked his hip and groaned deeply as Morgan stroked his chest. When they broke the kiss, Morgan kissed and sucked his way down his neck, sending glorious prickles of pleasure through him.

"I really thought this part of my life was over."

"I don't think so," Morgan told him with a wicked grin as he slid his hand down Richard's belly, sliding those magic fingers over his hips and then to his groin.

Richard held his breath until Morgan gripped his cock, stroking him firmly. There were times, early on, when Richard hadn't been sure if he'd ever be able to be sexual again.

Morgan met his gaze. "I intend to make you remember just how alive you are."

"Oh yeah?" Richard challenged, pulling himself out of his thoughts and back to Morgan. He needed to concentrate on the here and now and let the rest go.

"Yes." Morgan licked and then lightly bit his nipple.

Richard moaned softly, closing his eyes and sliding into the erotic energy. It had been so long since he'd been happy and could let go. Morgan made him feel safe, at least for the time being.

"Wait until you feel what I have for you." Morgan's wicked grin was back, and he held Richard's gaze, kissing his belly.

"What are you planning?"

"When was the last time you were sucked?" Morgan asked, and Richard quivered. "Not in some alley, but had someone take their time?"

Richard couldn't remember. He held his breath and let out a rumbly groan when Morgan's lips parted and he was surrounded by hot wetness that went deeper and took more of him.

This was so different from his encounters in the past. Each of Morgan's touches and the way he slowly moved up and down his shaft, tugging lightly, lips and tongue doing magic things, left Richard's head spinning. Morgan took him deep, sucking hard.

"God, that's good."

"You liked that?" Morgan asked with a proud grin.

"Hell yes!"

Morgan slowly took him deep again, holding him and then licking and sucking until Richard couldn't see straight. This was overwhelming.

Richard reached for Morgan, pulling him closer. He settled on the bed next to him, and Richard maneuvered as close as he could, then sucked Morgan's thick, heavy cock between his lips. Damn, this was heaven, sucking and being sucked. Surrounding someone and being surrounded at the same time. Richard was fast realizing he wasn't sure how much longer he was going to be able to hold off. The excitement building between them was becoming too intense to maintain.

"Richie," Morgan groaned softly.

He sucked harder in time to Morgan's thrilling ministrations. Soon they were moving together, groans and whimpers filling the room. It was like a chorus of care, and Richard was being carried away on its tones.

Pressure built deep inside him, and Richard knew he wasn't going to last much longer. Morgan felt too good around him, and Morgan's cock sliding faster and more intensely across his tongue revved him up even more. His body screamed for release, and Richard shook trying to hold back but gave up as Morgan reached his peak as well.

Richard swallowed, eyes clamped shut, as he came down Morgan's throat. It was wonderfully overwhelming and exciting.

Richard lay as still as he could, certain that this amazing feeling was as fragile as a soap bubble and the slightest movement would burst it. After a minute, Morgan pulled away. Richard expected him to leave, and all he could think about was how awkward it would be in the morning. But Morgan lay next to him, pulling up the covers.

"You know that things in the middle of the night can get difficult. Sometimes I have to get up, and it's never easy or pretty."

At least he didn't need catheters and things like that any longer. He'd really hated them.

"It's all right," Morgan said and slid his hand across Richard's belly, tugging them closer. "Just go to sleep, and if you need to get up, then get up. I'm not going anywhere."

Richard took him at his word and closed his eyes.

"RICHIE," MORGAN said at some point in the night.

"Huh?" He groaned and forced his eyes open. "What is it?"

"I'll be back. Call 911 and tell them there's someone outside the house."

Morgan rattled off the address, and Richard dialed the number while Morgan raced out of the room. A few seconds later, Morgan was turning on lights and running down the hallway. Light illuminated the window from outside as he did as Morgan requested. He told the operator they had a possible intruder and the address. She was calm and said someone was on their way. Richard told her he was in a wheelchair and had limited mobility. She offered to stay on the line with him, but Morgan returned, so he handed him the phone.

Morgan rattled off what he'd found and that the police and fire officials were needed. Then he hung up. "I scared him away, but he was preparing to do here what he did at your previous place."

"Gasoline?"

"Yeah. But he didn't get too far. The gate to the back creaks, and that's what woke me up. Turning on all the lights must have scared him off. The idiot left one of the cans—thank God it stayed upright."

"Do you think Angus will show up?"

"I don't know. But we need to be very careful and let them see what they can find. There may be prints or something on the can they can use."

"Do you want me to get up?" Richard asked, pushing up to a seated position.

"There really isn't any need. You were a big help making the call. I'll talk to the police and fire officials. They're going to want to look around and stuff."

Lights flashed on the hallway walls.

Richard lay back down. "If you need anything."

"Hopefully it won't take too long." Morgan sounded tired, and a knock on the front door had him hurrying out of the room.

Through the open door, Richard heard Morgan talking to what sounded like the police and then his fellow firemen as they left the house. Morgan was right, there was little Richard could do, but he sat up and got dressed since his clothes had been left within his reach, then transferred to his chair and rolled out to the kitchen. He knew where the coffee was, and he had a pretty good idea they were going to need some before the night was over.

"I thought you were in bed," Morgan said gently when he came back inside. "Oh gosh, coffee," Morgan groaned, and Richard poured him a mug.

"I thought you might want some. Are you finding anything out there?"

"No. The police are skeptical, but the firefighters are pretty convinced of what was happening." He took the mug. "I need to get back out there."

"I made a whole pot," Richard said.

"I'll tell them."

He left, and Richard glided into the living room. He wanted to know what was going on, but the stairs made that impossible. Richard grabbed a pillow and the throw from the sofa and got comfortable. Snippets of conversation reached his ears from outside, but mostly he waited.

"Morgan said you were up and to come inside," Angus said as he walked into the house, pulling Richard out of the doze he'd fallen into.

"Yeah." He pushed the pillow away but left the blanket draped over himself.

"Did you hear anything?"

"No. It was all Morgan. I was asleep, and Morgan woke me up and raced out of bed, asking me to call the police and stuff while he turned on lights. He said he scared the man away."

"It seems he did. But I wanted to talk to you about your friend."

"Do you think it was him?"

Angus shook his head. "No, unless he broke out of the mental hospital his family placed him in a year ago and managed to get here from Washington State. We tracked him down."

"All right, then why is someone doing this?"

"I don't know, but what's clear is that this guy has a method, and you're the common target for his attention. It could be a coincidence, but we really don't think so."

Now he was cold and pulled the blanket up higher. "What do you want me to tell you? I gave you the name of the guy I thought it could be."

"Is there anyone from before you were in the Marines?" Angus asked. "Someone who would hate you?"

"I was a teenager when I went into the Corps, and I spent almost ten years on active duty. That was my life for so very long, and I only moved back here after my parents died. It hasn't worked out too well. I did meet Morgan again, but… it seems I'm putting everyone around me in danger, and I have no idea why."

"All right," Angus said seriously. "Let's get closer. Is there someone you've really pissed off in the last few months? Did you run over someone's cat with your chair?"

"No." Richard chuckled. "I saw a few friends from high school a couple of weeks ago at the grocery store. They said hello. I did the same. The entire conversation lasted five minutes. There certainly wasn't something sinister at play. This is hateful and intended to cause hurt. It's deliberate, and I don't know of anyone who would have a reason to do this."

"Okay. But think it through. I can't help wondering if there's not something much more basic that we're missing. You were in the service, which means there are people out there who may not like you."

"Yeah, but most of them are in another part of the world, and I was just another faceless American." Richard felt completely helpless. "I really don't know what could have drawn this kind of attention."

"All right, but if you think of anything, let me know. I'm going to continue to work with the police. At the very least we have a serial arsonist on our hands, and we need to find him before he tries again. So anything you can think of, no matter how small, might help."

"You said he," Richard said.

"Arson is predominately a male crime." Angus said that as though it were a common fact. "All I'm asking is for you to be aware of the people around you. This guy has obviously followed you, so he's been around, watching you, and if you're vigilant, you might see him."

"He could have tried to burn the house down at any time," Richard said.

"Yes. But he tried in the middle of the night when you'd be asleep, just like last time. He wants to see you burn for whatever reason." Angus pulled up the footstool from the end of a wingback chair and sat near him. "Arson is a fantasy. For these guys it's kind of like sex. They love to see the flames and hear the roar. It fascinates them. But this guy is more than that. He wants to know that his enemies are being consumed along with the building. It isn't just about the fire."

"So he was likely watching the other night?" Richard asked.

"Probably. We took pictures of the people hanging around. There wasn't anyone tonight, but I'll bring pictures over to see if you recognize anyone. My police partner will run the MO through databases to see if we can come up with any possibilities, but it's a long shot. We had an arsonist a while ago, but we got him. Of course, you catch one and another pops up."

"How can you keep going after these guys like this?" Richard asked. "I mean, you have to start to think the way they do."

"Yeah. Sometimes it's a little scary in my head, but I have a good partner who helps bring me back to earth and keeps the bad things from taking over."

Angus smiled slightly. He was very attractive, and Kevin was a lucky man. Of course, he wasn't as handsome as Morgan, but that could just be his own particular opinion.

"I'll let you go back to bed. But please give it some thought, and be on the lookout. I'll bring by the pictures in the morning." Angus stood as Morgan came back inside. "Be sure to keep your eyes open."

"We will," Morgan said. "And we'll be in touch if we see anything." Morgan shook hands with Angus, and Richard did the same.

"Thanks for everything," Richard said and watched as Angus left the house. "Is it over for tonight?" Richard asked.

Morgan closed and locked the door. "Yes. All the gates are locked, and everything has been taken and marked for evidence. Apparently Angus gave the police quite a talking-to, and they now understand the extreme severity of what happened. They are going to have a car patrol the area for tonight to make sure we're undisturbed, but after that we need to keep our eyes open."

The flashing lights outside faded, and soon quiet reigned once again. Richard was having trouble keeping his eyes open and wished he'd had some coffee, but he had been hoping to get back to sleep. He put the throw on the arm of the sofa and wheeled back down to his room. He used the bathroom and then got undressed and back into bed. He wasn't sure if Morgan was going to join him again or not. Richard rolled onto his side and closed his eyes. He could hear Morgan's footsteps in the living room. Richard dozed off, falling deeper into sleep.

He woke with an arm around his waist and Morgan pressed to his back. Richard sighed happily and closed his eyes once again. "When did you join me?"

"A few hours ago?" Morgan whispered. "I couldn't go back to bed until I knew we were safe."

"So you stayed up all night?" Guilt bloomed inside him.

"I dozed on the sofa but jumped at every noise. I wasn't sure if they were going to try again." Morgan tightened his hug and grew quiet. "I need to sleep for a while."

"Aren't you hungry?"

Richard was waking, and sleep wasn't going to come again. Morgan didn't answer. Richard carefully got into his chair and pulled on sweats before leaving the room. He wheeled down into the kitchen, dumped out the pot of coffee he'd made during the night, and started a fresh pot. Then he checked out the refrigerator, finding some eggs and bacon. He also found some bread and butter. Richard got to work making breakfast. He found a way to lift himself up enough to be able to make the eggs. He cooked the bacon in the oven on a cookie sheet and then found a tray on the counter and made up a large plate, getting the dishes from the dishwasher, which was thankfully clean. He put the plate on the tray along with a thermos of coffee and two mugs before carefully making his way down the hall.

"Morgan," he said softly and watched Morgan's eyes crack open as the scent of coffee called to him.

"Oh God, that smells good," Morgan moaned.

"I'm going to need your help. I can bring you the breakfast, but I can't get it up to you."

There was only so much he was able to do without spilling coffee and food everywhere. Morgan walked around the bed and lifted the tray off his lap. Then Richard went back around to the side of the bed and joined Morgan.

"This was very nice of you," Morgan said as they sat side by side, munching on pieces of bacon. "It was what I needed." He poured a mug of coffee for each of them. "You make really good eggs. They're nice and fluffy."

"Thanks." At least he was good for something. "Would it be all right to see Grace and her family? I can call and find out where they are, but I want to make sure they're okay." The guilt had settled heavily on him during the night. They had lost their home because of him, and he had to try to do something to make it right. Not that he ever could, but he needed to be there for them. He set down his bacon, appetite now gone.

"Of course." Morgan carefully shifted. "You know that none of this is your fault."

Richard shook his head. "That's easy for you to say. But this *is* my fault. Someone is after me, and because of that they lost their home, and you could have lost yours." Richard had to know. "Why haven't you told me to go? You should, you know. It would be much safer for you if I were to leave, and then you wouldn't be sitting up all night."

Morgan set down his fork and wiped his mouth. "Regardless of what anyone believes, it's premature to say that you are the cause of this. This could be a coincidence or someone who is after me or my attention somehow. Until we catch this bastard, we aren't going to know, and I'm going to kill Angus if he led you to believe you were at fault. There's a lot none of us knows, and yes, you may seem to be the common denominator, but that's all at this point." He picked up his fork once again.

"But...."

"Friends don't push friends away when things get hard."

"But we've barely seen each other in twenty years," Richard protested.

Morgan set the tray that rested on his lap on the bed and slowly got up. Richard did his best not to watch his incredibly white bare ass as it bounced slightly with each step but failed miserably. Morgan left the room, returning with a box made of rough wood that looked as though it had been polished by years of handling. He opened it and took something out, then closed the box and returned to the bed. "Hold out your hand."

Richard did, and Morgan dropped something cool into it. A small black ring, fashioned out of a nail, rested in his hand. "What's this?"

"It should be familiar. We both had one. Amy gave them to us when we were kids."

Richard's mouth fell open slightly. "It can't be."

"Yes, it is. This was my wedding ring from when Amy married us when we were thirteen. It was a few weeks before my father moved us away."

"That was just pretend," Richard said, still holding the small piece of metal.

"I know that. But I still have the ring." Morgan took it back and held it tightly in his hand. "I kept that ring after I left. It was part of what I had of you. The box had been my mother's, and it's where I keep what's special to me, and that ring has been inside since just after the day it was given to me."

"I don't understand." What was Morgan getting at? Richard couldn't believe that after all these years Morgan had actually kept that ring. He tried to think of what had happened to his. It might be in among the things he had in storage from his parents. He wasn't sure. Richard had kept what was truly important, and the rest the executor had sold on his behalf.

"I wanted you to know that I still had it and that I valued the friendship we had enough to carry it with me." He leaned over, lightly touching Richard's chin, sending a zing through his jaw. "I didn't go to bed with you last night because of when we were kids. I did it because I like you. The man you are now."

"Are you sure?" Richard asked. "You don't need to be acting on some overly sensitive sense of duty."

Morgan's eyes darkened. "I don't sleep with people out of duty, and for that matter I don't do it out of pity or charity either. I have a heart, and I know it and what I want. So you can stop thinking all the crap that's going through your head right now."

"Okay." Richard acquiesced, but he was still finding it hard to believe what Morgan was saying. He wanted to smack himself on the side of the head. Why was he having so much trouble thinking that someone could be nice to him and care for him? "I'll take you at your word."

That seemed to make Morgan happy, and they finished eating. Then he took the tray away, put the ring back in the box, and got back under the covers.

"Do you want to rest for a while?" Richard asked.

Morgan grinned and tugged him close. "Resting is on the list, eventually."

Richard rolled onto his side, and Morgan guided them together until their legs and chests pressed to one another. "I see."

"No. I don't think you do, but I hope you will. I have had sex because it was what I needed at the time, but it was always hollow and cold afterwards. Being with you is all heat and fire." Morgan caressed his cheek and then trailed a thumb over his lips. "It feels right to me, like this was meant to be somehow."

"I don't know if I believe in things like that."

"I do."

"The things I've seen…." Richard closed his eyes. "It isn't possible for there to be some power that controls the fates and predestines things like that. If there were, then…." He couldn't talk about this. Not now when he had Morgan in his arms. He didn't want to taint someone's wonderful feelings with memories that were as black as the darkest coal.

"I'm only telling you what it is that I feel and what I've known for quite a while."

Richard blinked and held still. "I keep waiting for the other shoe to drop."

"Why?"

"Because it always does. And let's face it, this is too damned good to be true."

Morgan nodded slowly. "I think you're right. Maybe I am expecting too much."

"I like that you expect things, but I'm not sure I can meet your expectations." Richard pushed away the covers. "Look at me, Morgan, really look at me. My legs can't move on their own. I can feel them, but there's no strength, and there never will be. There was too much damage, so I'm going to be in the chair for the rest of my life, and there's nothing I can do about it."

"So you're going to give up?"

"God, you can be so sanctimonious. I'm not giving up, but I also don't expect everyone I meet to be able to deal with that. I'm realistic, and you have your head in the clouds." Richard looked back to Morgan. "I can't even get out of this house on my own." That sent a jolt of fear through him. He hadn't really thought about that, but it was true. He was stuck in this house unless he was willing to go down the stairs on his butt and then roll or pull himself across the yard.

"That's a new one," Morgan said rather darkly.

"To you everything is easy and clear. It isn't to me." Richard sat up. He needed a minute. "I had just arrived on the first overseas assignment, and of course I was in Iraq. Dreadful place. I knew I was going either there or Afghanistan when I signed up, but I had no idea what it was like until I got there. I was assigned to guard one of the bases. It should have been a relatively easy assignment. The base wasn't even in a volatile area. But we were targeted the second night, and a local man approached. It wasn't even dark. He said something to one of the other guys, and then he just exploded. Guts and body parts went everywhere. The other guy from my unit, I hadn't had a chance to learn more than his name, was dead, and I had been knocked on my ass. He was as green as I was, and now, after two days, he was dead." Richard inhaled to steady himself. "That was my indoctrination. The guy that approached was known to a lot of the other men. He was a man from a nearby village, nice family, ones that we'd helped."

"Then what happened?"

"Apparently his family had been taken hostage, and the price for their lives was his. He strapped a bomb to himself and blew himself up for them." Richard kept the anger and hatred in its little box inside him, but just barely. "See, there is so much more to everything than it appears. Nothing is black-and-white, not even when someone dies."

Andrew Grey

"I think I see," Morgan said.

"No you don't. See, if I'd been in the same situation and someone had my mom and dad, I probably would have done the exact same thing." He dared a glance into Morgan's eyes and saw fear mixed with something he didn't understand. "You never know what's in someone until you press them. Black, white, gray, they all mix together. I thought that life outside the Corps would be easy, but it's harder. There's no structure, no one giving orders and doing the master planning. It's just a free-for-all."

"Then maybe that's why I leave some things to fate and worry about what's in my control," Morgan said. "I'm not a kid, and I've been around." Morgan took his hand, which was an unexpected gesture. "Believe it or not, I've seen my own version of combat. I may not have been in the military, but I've seen things that have stuck with me for years."

Richard leaned back against the headboard, skeptical as hell, but he listened.

"I had been on the force a year, maybe a little longer, and we were called to a fire in an apartment building. It was old and matchstick dry. The dang thing went up quick. By the time we got there, most of the place was involved, but the apartments on the end were clear, so I was assigned to go in along with another firefighter and get the people out. Tim Dryer and I went in and made our way through the smoke-filled hallway and broke down the doors. We got inside just as the fire breached the walls of the apartment. We raced for the bedrooms and found three kids. I took two, and he took the older one, and we made a mad dash out of the building with the fire chasing us the entire way. As soon as we got out, I handed the kids to EMTs and they got to work. Tim did the same, and then we were checked over because of the heat. Both of us were fine, but…."

"Did the parents make it out?"

Morgan shook his head. "They were in the room we couldn't reach in time. And two of the little boys, the ones I carried out,

80

were already dead. They had breathed in too much toxic smoke. The third did survive, but he was alone." Morgan wiped his eyes.

"Is he the first rescue victim you visited in the hospital?" Richard didn't know where that question came from, but he knew he was right.

"Yes. I visited him every day until he was discharged and his aunt took him home with her. He's in college now, and I get the occasional e-mail from him. But sometimes I still see his brothers in my dreams, and I wonder if I could have been faster or… something."

"If I'd spoken up and told Alan to be wary…," Richard said. "The what-ifs are what run through my head all the time. I see the guys who were killed and wonder what if I'd been faster or if my shot had been more accurate. My therapists said that came with the territory and that there was little I could do about it other than accept that things happen outside of my control." Richard huffed. "Which is total bullshit, because no matter what I do, at night, I see the same things over and over again, and I'm always too late or my shot isn't good enough, again and again." Richard rested back and closed his eyes. "How in hell did we get on this depressing topic?"

"You can't escape your past," Morgan said.

"No. But I wish to hell I didn't relive it over and over again. That part really sucks." He pushed back the covers and slid out of the bed and back into his chair. He made a mental note that delving into the past was a surefire way to kill the mood as he got some of the clothes that Morgan had gotten for him. He put them on his lap and wheeled across the hall. "I won't be long."

"And I'll take care of the dishes," Morgan called.

"Sorry. I can do them when I've finished dressing." He closed the bathroom door, needing a few minutes alone. He hated talking about the past and all those things he remembered and wished to hell he hadn't. Maybe someday he'd be lucky enough to get hit on the head and could come down with a good case of amnesia.

"Just come on out when you're done," Morgan called through the door.

Richard washed up and went through the process of getting dressed and putting on his shoes. Morgan was dressed and waiting for him by the time he came out of the bathroom.

"Call Grace and see what's going on with her, and then I was thinking that we could make a stop at Home Depot. I need to get some building supplies so we can put a ramp at the front door so you can get in and out of the house on your own. There are only a few steps, so it doesn't have to be a huge project, but I want you to be able to come and go."

"What about the house? Will this guy try again?" Richard asked.

"There isn't much I can do if he does. We can't sit here watching the house all the time. I'll have to go to work, and I'm sure you have things you need to do. We should also get your car and make sure that's okay. I'm sure you'd like to be able to drive yourself where you need to go."

"I sort of like having a chauffeur," Richard wisecracked. "But I'll need my car. It's old, but the VA helped me get it outfitted so I can drive it."

"Go on and make your call. I'll finish up the dishes, and then we can go."

Morgan went back to the kitchen, and Richard called Grace. They had found temporary housing, and she gave him the address. By the time he was done, Morgan was ready to go.

He'd been dreading visiting the old house, and it was everything he expected. As soon as he got close, the smell of smoke and burned wood assaulted his nose. Morgan helped with his chair, and he slowly propelled himself toward the door of his former home. There was very little left. "It looks like the burned-out buildings in Iraq."

Morgan peered in through one of the now-empty window openings. "There isn't anything on the inside. It's just a shell now."

Richard had been hoping there would be something salvageable, but that seemed hopeless. A few birds fluttered around, but they didn't stay long. It was like an air of despair surrounded the place now. "You mentioned getting my car, but I don't have any keys. They were inside the apartment."

"Okay. Let's get the make and model along with the VIN number and key codes. That should be enough for them to make another set for you." Morgan checked his watch. "We should go meet Grace."

They went back to the car, and Richard was so glad to leave. The drive to Grace's apartment took only a few minutes. They were on the fourth floor, and Richard took the elevator. When he got out, the door was open, and the kids hurried to greet him, surrounding him in hugs and worried laughter.

"Let Richard come inside," Grace said, and he made his way into the apartment. It was small and furnished in early boring industrial furniture. Sort of what a corporate flunky thought to put in the place.

"I'm so sorry, Grace," Richard said when he couldn't stand it anymore. She bent down to hug him. "They think it has something to do with me."

"It has to do with the nutcase who set our house on fire," Grace told him. "So you put all that guilt out of your head. Billy wouldn't want that, and neither do I."

By now she was crying, and Richard was seconds away from it too. Thankfully she pulled away and turned to wipe her nose and face.

"This is Morgan. He's the firefighter who rescued me, and it turns out, an old friend I knew from years ago. Morgan, this is Grace and her son, Devon, and daughter, Michelle." Devon was eight and Michelle six. He was so relieved they got out unscathed. They all said hello but still seemed a little shell-shocked, which probably wasn't surprising. "I wanted to come and see how you were doing."

"The insurance company has us set up here, and they've given us some money, so I've been able to replace some of the kids' things and make them a little comfortable. It looks like the house is a total loss, so they'll probably have us house hunting soon." She clearly wasn't ready for any of what was ahead, judging by the way her lower lip quivered.

"It'll be all right," he said, hugging her once again. The kids played on the floor, and Grace motioned Richard and Morgan inside and toward the sofa.

"Can I get you anything?"

Richard shook his head.

"No, thank you," Morgan said. "Richie was concerned about how you all were doing."

"The police and fire investigators have talked to me a few times, but we don't know anything. I just hope this is over and that we can go back to what's become normal. Everything is so turned upside down and has been for so long."

"I know," Richard said. "Nothing is ever going to be the same, but we all have to move on."

Grace wiped her eyes. "One of our old neighbors has been here every day to help us. He's taken the kids to the park and gotten them ice cream and stuff to get them out a few times." She dried her tears. "He even asked if I would go to dinner. I think he likes me, but...."

"You know it's okay to go on with your life. Billy would want that more than anything. I know you lost him, but the last thing he'd want is for you and the kids to stop living. I think that would be like hurting him all over again. He loved you all so much and showed us all the pictures you sent. He was proud of his family, and there's no need to grieve for him that way."

"After the kids' father turned out to be a jerk, Billy was there for us. Even when he was deployed, we knew he was in our corner."

"Was your neighbor the man who was with you the night of the fire?" Morgan asked.

"Yes. He saw the smoke and banged on the door to wake us up. I got the kids up and out right away. I guess he saved our lives." Her smile seemed forced, and she wiped her eyes again. "I guess it's time I stopped all this grieving, and maybe I will go out with Gary." She seemed happier but still held Richard's hand.

"Mom, can we go outside?" Devon asked.

"Sure. Just stay in the yard in front, and don't go any farther than the sidewalk," she told them both, and they hurried out of the apartment, staying close together. "I swear Devon hasn't slept since the fire. He's afraid and says if he does, then maybe the apartment will catch fire, and Michelle keeps asking for the things she lost in the fire. How am I supposed to replace the pictures of them as babies or the doll she had on her bed and slept with since she was four?"

Richard had no answers for her. "I keep thinking that it'll get better. I suggest you ask family and friends to look and see if they have pictures. If they do they can send them or make copies. It won't replace what you lost, but it will give you something, and who knows what you'll find."

"Thank you." She hugged him again and then went to the window to check on the kids.

Richard turned to Morgan, who seemed to understand what he wanted.

"We should be going. I've got to get some things so I can build a ramp for Richie. He's staying with me, and maybe you and the kids could come over next weekend. We could cook out, and they could run in the backyard all they want."

"That's so nice. Thank you," Grace said with a huge smile, and they headed for the door. She was becoming agitated, and as soon as the door was closed, Richard rolled to the elevator.

"She's had all she can take right now."

Morgan nodded. "I've seen so many people who have lost everything, and it's usually the same. They never lament the loss of the house or the things that can be replaced. It's always the things that were in the house that hold memories for them. It's like the fire

85

burned up part of their past." Morgan rested his hand on Richard's shoulder as the elevator descended. "You were wonderful with her, and that was a great suggestion."

"Thanks." He'd seen too much loss not to have been affected by it. Before he could say anything, the elevator doors opened, and he rolled out of the lobby and to the front yard. At the same time, he saw Grace and the kids exit the building via the staircase. They began playing some version of a chase game. They laughed and ran on the grass. Richard stopped and watched them for a minute or so before continuing down the walk before he could think too long and hard about how he'd never be able to do that again. "Home Depot next?" he asked.

"Yeah." They got in the car, and after waving good-bye, headed out to the store.

RICHARD SAT watching as Morgan worked. He had to admit that, while he was doing what he could to help, Morgan had worked up a sweat and had taken off his shirt a little while ago. Richard measured the two-by-four for Morgan and had to do it again because he found his mind was on other things, like the way Morgan's chest had felt against his. Damn, the man was sex on a stick. Morgan stretched to get a pencil, and Richard groaned as he wheeled closer, running his hands over the acres of taut, firm muscle.

"I'm never going to get this done if you do that," Morgan said.

"Yeah, well, with you running around half naked, I can't seem to measure anything at all."

"I should put my shirt back on, then," Morgan said and reached to where he'd draped the white T-shirt over the porch railing.

"Don't you dare! It's the perks that make this job special." He wheeled closer. "And you are the best perk ever."

He leaned upward so they could share a kiss. Then Morgan went back to work, and Richard forced his mind onto the task at hand.

A truck pulled into the drive, and Angus got out, with a much smaller man walking around to meet him.

"Hey, Kevin." Morgan set down his tools.

"Is now a good time? I wanted to show Richie the pictures to see if he recognizes anyone."

"It's fine." He wiped his hands on a rag and shook hands with both of them. Richard did the same.

"You go with Richie, and I'll help Morgan," Kevin said.

Richard wheeled over to the makeshift table that Morgan had set up for him while the other two got to work.

"I hope he's almost done. I swear he's building the Eiffel Tower of wheelchair ramps."

"Morgan never does anything by halves," Angus said as he laid out the printed photographs. "Usually I do this electronically, but if you saw anyone you recognized, we can note it right on the picture."

Angus stepped back, and Richard perused the pictures and then picked up each, one by one.

"There's no one in this one I recognize," he said, handing it back to Angus before moving on to the next one. "This is mostly the firefighters." He looked closely. "There are some people too far out of range to be seen clearly." He took another and scanned it closely before passing that one with a shake of his head.

"Wait," he said, examining the next one. "This guy looks familiar."

"That's the family who owned the house. I included it mostly for the people behind them."

"Yeah. Is there a close-up of them?" he asked, and Angus looked over the pictures that remained and handed one to him. "Oh, they're just neighbors. I know some of them, but only because they live nearby." He didn't think it would be any of them.

"Were there any fights or disagreements with the neighbors?"

"Not that I'm aware of." Richard looked up from the photograph. "Burning someone's house down would be a little extreme for a disagreement."

"That's extreme, period, and you never know."

"I suppose." He handed the photograph back and continued looking. "I don't see anyone I recognize. I mean, there are people I know, but none of them are out of place. There isn't some blast from my past hiding in the shadows. That's Grace, her family, and the neighbor. He likes her, but Grace isn't sure she's ready. I'd expect him to be there, just like I'd expect the rest of the neighbors too." He handed back the last pictures. "Did they get anything from last night?"

"There were prints on the gas can, but most were very smudged and deteriorated. They did get some, though, and they're working on it. Mostly we're not coming up with much, and though we're really trying to find a way to tie the two incidents together, we're coming up with zilch." Angus gathered the pictures. "It was a long shot. If I were going to do this, I'd stay in the background as best I could, but you never know."

"I wasn't there," Kevin called over.

"I know, eagle eyes," Angus said right back and then turned to him. "Kevin has this ability to see things and infer things from pictures and video that others miss. I had him look at the pictures, and he didn't see anything either. He once recognized someone in a video from his shoes."

"They were cool shoes," Kevin said as he held a sheet of plywood while Morgan cut it.

"So where do we go from here?" Richard asked.

"He's going to strike again somewhere, and probably soon. He was stopped, and the need to see something burn is going to build up. So keep your eyes and ears open." Angus turned to where Morgan was now positioning the cut board on the deck of the ramp. "Maybe you should consider getting a dog. I have a friend who has a couple of pups. They're six months old, and they need homes." Angus turned back and winked.

"You have to be kidding. With the schedule I work? What am I supposed to do while I'm away all day?"

"We have a dog walker," Kevin said. "She comes in and lets Mitzy go out and do her business. She takes her for a walk and sees that she's okay. Then I walk her when I get home."

"Mitzy?" Morgan asked.

"Yeah. Kevin loved the name. She's a sixty-pound German shepherd."

Angus was clearly amused. Kevin walked over to the truck and opened the back door. A huge dog bounded out, wriggling around Angus.

"Mitzy, sit," Kevin said, and she dropped in place, watching him with adoration. "Stay there, and be good."

She panted and didn't move. Richard wheeled over and held out his hand. Mitzy sniffed it and licked his fingers but didn't move, watching Kevin.

"She thinks Kevin walks on water and pees champagne. We got her at a rescue, and she and Kevin bonded within seconds. He taught her to mind, and she'll do anything he says."

"You can say hello to Richie, but be good, and no jumping."

Mitzy stood and let Richard pet her, soaking up the attention. Richard didn't want to ask Morgan about a dog because this wasn't his home, and he had no right to mention it.

"You're a good girl, aren't you?" he asked. She rested her head on his lap, big brown eyes looking up at him.

"You'd think we ignored her all the time," Angus said.

Kevin went back to work, and Richard petted Mitzy's head until she started when Morgan started sawing again. Angus comforted her until the whine of the saw faded away. Richard backed his chair a little farther away, and Mitzy went with him. This time she wasn't as nervous when the saw started once again.

He sat minding the dog and staying out of the way while Morgan finished the ramp.

"That's going to hold really well," Kevin said as he walked back and forth up and down the ramp.

It was steady, and more than once Richard wondered why Morgan hadn't arranged for some temporary ramp. It wasn't like he was going to be staying here forever. He would need to get his own place and move on with his life, just like Morgan would. Besides, it was only a matter of time before the PTSD and the bother of living with someone in a chair got to Morgan and he'd have to move on.

Mitzy's barking pulled him out of his thoughts. She raced up and down the ramp, then sat at the top as though she were the queen and her subjects had to come to her on their knees.

"Are you ready to try it out?" Morgan asked, leaning close to him from behind.

Sweat and the hint of aftershave reached Richard's nose, quickening his heartbeat. Morgan's tone was a little breathy and seductive.

"You have to know that I built this just for you."

"I know…," he answered, turning to see him and getting a stronger whiff of musk that sent a tremble running down his spine and settling in his groin. It didn't help that heat from Morgan's bare skin went right through the T-shirt Richard was wearing.

"I want to make sure you can make it up and down on your own."

Morgan moved closer, and Richard wanted everyone gone so that when he made it to the top, he could continue inside and down the hall, leading Morgan right into the bedroom. Morgan pushed him to the base of the ramp and then stepped back. Damn it. Maybe if he feigned some sort of distress, he'd be able to elicit some help from Morgan. Of course, that wasn't going to help him.

Richard got to it, propelling himself forward. The ramp wasn't too long or too high. He made it to the top and turned around, then glided down.

"I take it you're a speed demon," Angus said.

"Yeah, I was," Richard said. "I used to be the one who drove like a bat out of hell. I was the one in the unit who figured out that you could get a Humvee airborne under the right circumstances."

He chuckled. "I don't recommend it. The Marine with me puked his guts out after we came to a stop. Grant never rode with me again under any circumstances. I don't do things like that any longer."

"I should hope not," Morgan chastised. "Does it work?"

"It's perfect. I can get up and down easily." He still wondered why Morgan had gone to so much trouble and expense.

"Great." Morgan began gathering up the tools. "I was going to get cleaned up and then go to dinner. Do you want to go with us?"

Richard turned to where Angus stood next to Kevin, an arm around his shoulders. Mitzy stood near Kevin's feet, looking up at him like she wanted in on the hugs. They looked so happy, and he wanted to feel that exact same way. Then Richard turned to Morgan, who was looking at him, his expression nearly identical to Angus's. That's what he didn't understand. Why would Morgan look at him like that? It had to be some misplaced sense of old friendship. They really hadn't known each other long enough for Morgan to have those huge deer eyes when he looked at him. Something was most definitely wrong with this picture. He could imagine Angus watching Kevin like that. Kevin was cute, and he was whole, and he had so much energy that it lit up the very air around him. Richard wasn't like that at all. If anything, he was the black hole that sucked away others' light. Half a man with only half a future.

Richard turned away and heard Morgan go inside. He'd been deep enough in thought that he hadn't heard Angus's answer to Morgan's question, but from the fact that they were still here and the way Kevin took off across the yard with Mitzy right behind him, it looked like they intended to join him and Morgan for dinner.

"Mitzy," Richard called.

She looked at Kevin, who pointed in his direction, and Mitzy took off across the yard. Richard figured he'd just become a target and was probably going to go flying when she barreled into him, but she pulled to a stop, tail wagging a mile a minute. Richard ran his fingers through her coat, and she soaked in the attention.

"Did you have a dog growing up?" Kevin asked as he approached.

"No. My dad never let me have one." Even as an adult, he'd never thought of getting a dog. His military life hadn't allowed for it, and he'd never thought of it after his discharge.

"You should get one. There are organizations that place helper dogs. They're trained to walk alongside wheelchairs and be an extra set of eyes in addition to providing companionship. The dogs from these organizations are well tempered and trained. So you don't have to try to teach them everything from scratch. You might think about it."

"I will," Richard said, but he didn't really mean it. Sure, he'd like a dog, but most of the time he struggled to take care of himself, let alone a dog. "She's such a good girl."

"Mitzy's really special. I know she wasn't treated very well before. She's smart and loves to learn new things. I'm going to take her to a dog training school. They'll teach her balance and even more discipline."

"Like tricks?" Richard asked skeptically.

"No. More like things that will exercise her mind. She's very inquisitive, so if she can keep learning, she'll be happier. Some dogs are like people. If they stop learning and growing, they become bored." Kevin knelt next to Mitzy. "We don't want that for you, do we? You're the most amazing dog ever."

He hugged her and then took off with Mitzy right behind him. Angus joined them, and Richard watched, sitting on the sidelines the way he seemed to for most things.

There had to be a place where he fit in. Maybe it was time to contact the VA and see about going back. He didn't need to be a weight on the lives of everyone around him. God, he didn't want to be around himself. The worst thing about being in the chair had to be the fact that he'd been relegated to onlooker status. Others played and laughed while he sat and watched.

The front door smacked closed, and Richard turned as Morgan walked down the ramp. "Are you ready to go to dinner?"

Richard wheeled closer. "Morgan, I'm not feeling very well. I can stay here with Mitzy while the three of you eat. I'll have a sandwich and lie down for a while."

"Are you sick? Have you done too much? I should have made sure you took it easier."

"No. I'm a little wiped out, I think." He was feeling depressed and knew he'd only bring down everyone at dinner. It was best if he stayed away, rested, and maybe made some phone calls so he could try to find somewhere to go. He couldn't sponge off Morgan any longer. He turned around and saw the ramp. Morgan had been so nice and had built it just for him. He clamped his eyes closed. That thought added to his own misery. He'd let Morgan go to all this trouble and expense, and he was only a guest. What did that say about him? Morgan was kind and thoughtful to a fault, and he'd taken advantage of that. That alone made him a pretty selfish and useless person.

"Are you sure? I don't want to push you, but…." Morgan paused. "I shouldn't push. Why don't I help you inside?"

"I can do it," Richard said and made his way up the ramp and inside the house. He didn't dare turn around. He felt Morgan's steps retreat. Once inside, Richard transferred to the sofa. Kevin came in a few minutes later with Mitzy.

"Are you sure it's okay to leave her with you?" Kevin asked.

"Of course." Richard stroked her head.

"I'll put a bowl of water down for her," Morgan said.

They fussed for a few minutes, and then Morgan came over.

"You know where everything is, so help yourself if you get hungry."

"Have a good time with your friends. I'm just going to rest." He reached for the throw from the back of the sofa and spread it over his legs. "Please don't worry—I'll be fine."

"Are you sure? I can tell Kevin and Angus that we'll go to dinner another time."

"Just go and have some fun." It seemed to Richard as though he was going to kill the evening whether he went or not. "I promise I'll be fine." He smiled as best he could for Morgan's benefit.

Morgan left a little while later. Richard wasn't sure if Mitzy was supposed to be up on the furniture, but once they were alone, she climbed onto the sofa, settling near his feet and resting her head on his leg. The house was quiet and empty. He had expected to feel alone but not empty, as though he had just pushed away something—or someone—he hadn't realized was precious to him until he was gone, and what really bothered Richard was that look on Morgan's face when he left. Some of the light was gone from his eyes, and Richard wasn't sure how to put it back—or even if he could.

Chapter 5

"THAT WAS something else," Henry said as they got down from the truck after spending hours at a fire.

They were all covered in sweat and soot. The fire had been at a facility with a lot of paper, apparently it was records storage, so the amount of ash had been unbelievable.

"Tell me about it," Morgan groaned.

"Ayers, you have a visitor," the captain on duty said. "Go on up now."

"Thanks." He got out of his fire clothes and hurried upstairs, where he found Angus waiting for him. "Have you been waiting long?"

"No. I left your captain a message, and he called when you were on your way back." They went into the conference room and closed the door. "I have some news for you. We did get a good print from the gas can that was left at your house, but we don't have a match to anyone at the moment. Antonio and I are working to widen our search for an identity, but it's very slow going."

Morgan nodded. "I appreciate that, but you could have just called."

"I know. I also wanted to see how things were with Richie."

Morgan shrugged. "I have no idea. I can feel him pulling away. He's quiet and keeping mostly to himself." He didn't go into details, like that Richie had taken to going to bed early and closing his door. "I keep wondering what I did. He's making calls to try to find an apartment of his own, and in a way I can't blame him for that."

"I take it you don't want him to leave," Angus said.

"No. I like having him there. You know how nice it is to come home to a house that isn't empty and to have someone happy to see you."

Skepticism filled Angus's eyes. "Is that the only reason you want him there? Because if it is, then Richie's doing the right thing."

"No, it isn't," Morgan answered forcefully.

"Then maybe you can explain it to me. This is someone you haven't seen in years and just met again when you rescued him during a fire a week ago. I don't understand the attachment you have to him."

Morgan stood up and walked to the window. "I can't explain it either. I saw Richie again, and everything felt right. It's like he's the other half of me. I just know it."

"Okay. Let's say you're right. Are you the other half of him?" Angus asked. "Just because you feel something doesn't mean he does. And Richie has been through a lot—it's written on his face and on his body. He isn't going to accept things as easily as you seem to."

"But…."

"Just think about it. I could be wrong, but he needs to know something, and I wish I could tell you what it is."

"Thanks. You've been a big help."

"I don't have all the answers. You need to flounder in the dark the same as the rest of us. But if you want my advice, talk to him, really talk, and that means you should be letting him do most of the talking and you should listen, not just to what he's saying, but what he's trying to tell you. They may be different things." Angus got up to leave. "And both of you keep your eyes open. It's been quiet, which means the pressure is building up in our guy, and he'll blow eventually."

"We are," Morgan assured him.

They hugged before Angus opened the door and left the room. Morgan closed it behind him and sat in one of the chairs. He honestly thought he'd shown Richie how he felt. But maybe they did need a chance to talk. Morgan checked the clock and was pleased that his shift would be over in a few hours and he could go home. Mostly it would be to sleep, but he'd be sure to talk to Richie before he went to bed.

The alarm went off, and he sprang into action, not having a chance to think about anything else for a few hours until he returned to the station even more exhausted than he'd been before. He gathered his things and drove home on autopilot.

The house was dark, and that worried Morgan until he parked in the drive behind Richie's car. They'd been able to get new keys made for it, and Richie had brought it to the house. Morgan grabbed his bag and went inside the silent house. It wasn't late enough for Richie to be in bed. Morgan turned on the lights and found Richie sitting at the kitchen table asleep in his chair. He woke him gently, then took his bag into the laundry room, where he started a load before returning to the kitchen.

"Are you all right?"

"I'm fine," Richie answered quickly. "I spent most of the day out looking at apartments. Well, looking at buildings mostly. I couldn't get inside many of the buildings, so there was no use in me going any farther. Even ground-floor places seem to have stairs."

"You know you don't need to be in a hurry," Morgan told him. "I like having you here."

It was clear Richie didn't believe him. "I need to be on my own."

How could he argue with Richie, regardless of his own feelings? Angus was right. Just because he felt a certain way didn't mean Richie felt the same. "If that's what you want."

"Isn't it what you want? You need to go back to your life without me hanging like an anchor around your neck. I know you like me and all, but you shouldn't place your life on hold because of me."

"Did I say I was putting my life on hold?" Morgan challenged.

"Of course not. You'd never do that. Instead, you'd let me stay here for months and never say a thing because you're that nice."

The pain in Richie's voice was hard for him to understand. Was Richie trying to say that he was too nice?

"Like I'd let that happen," Morgan scoffed. "You seem to think I'm some kind of pushover. I'm not, and if I wanted you to go, I'd say so. But you're free to do what you want. I've tried to make my home inviting and open for you. Not because I feel sorry for you but because you are who you are." Morgan's head ached, and he was so damned tired he could barely stand up. "So if you want to go, then do. If you wish to stay, you're welcome to do that too." He wanted to say that if Richie wanted to share his bed, that would be amazing, but this wasn't the time for that kind of discussion. At least he didn't think it was. Mostly these last few days had been confusing for him. "You say you want people to see more than the chair. But maybe it's you who needs to see past the chair." Morgan turned and walked back out the front door and into the yard. He needed fresh air and a chance to think before he said something he'd regret.

The chill in the night air cooled his temper. He could have used the sounds of the night he remembered as a kid. They were mostly obscured by cars and the wind, but occasionally the sound of crickets came forward when the city held its breath and remained silent for a few seconds.

The area around him grew brighter, and he turned around. Richie had turned on another light in the house and sat at the window watching him. Morgan went back inside, climbing the ramp and opening the door.

"I don't understand you," Richie said as Morgan stepped into the living room.

Morgan shrugged. "Maybe because you're trying to find a complex answer when the most obvious one is staring you in the face." That could be his answer as well. Maybe Richie simply didn't feel the same way he did and needed to get away. If that was the case, then Morgan had to step back and let Richie go no matter what his heart told him to do. The ball was in Richie's court, and all

Morgan could do was wait. "I need to go to bed, because otherwise I'm going to fall over."

He didn't try to kiss Richie. Instead he went to the laundry room and shoved the load of wash into the dryer. Then he went to the bathroom, cleaning up and showering off the grime and dirt before crawling into his own bed. Morgan wished he weren't alone, but so be it. He wasn't going to force himself on Richie or anyone. But damn, he missed those little quivering muscles with each touch and the way Richie gasped in surprise whenever he was supremely happy, as though he never expected to be that way again. What thrilled him most was that he'd been making those sounds for Morgan. Well, not anymore.

Morgan always thought that the best way to build a relationship and make someone care for you was to try to make them happy. He'd done everything he could think of to do that for Richie. Maybe that was the issue. Richie didn't want to be happy. He was content wallowing in his misery and depression, which was really sad, but there was nothing Morgan could do to change that. Whatever happened, it had to come from inside Richie. Morgan was realizing he couldn't do it for him or even nudge him in the direction he wanted. It sucked, because he wanted to help. Talk about frustration.

He rolled onto his side and closed his eyes. Morgan was too bone weary to remain awake for very long. At one point he might have heard Richie in the hallway, but he was too tired to really pay close attention and fell into a deep but active sleep. He woke hours later, twisted in the covers. After getting up, he got a drink and straightened the bed before getting back into it.

"Morgan," Richie said from his room as he was walking back to bed.

"Are you all right?" Morgan asked, completely forgetting he wasn't wearing anything.

"Just thirsty," Richie answered, and Morgan returned to the bathroom and brought Richie a fresh glass of water. He handed it to him and waited for him to drink, then took the empty glass.

"Is there something else you'd like?" He placed the glass on the bedside table and leaned closer. "I can feel the heat rolling off you."

Richie swallowed. "I...."

"The question I think you have to answer is what do you want? Nothing else matters. Don't worry about what everyone else is thinking. Just ask yourself what it is that you want. Then reach out and take it."

"But what if I can't have it?" Richie asked.

"What if you can?" Morgan leaned even closer and then held still, his lips inches from Richie's, but that last little way, that was a journey Richie had to make. Morgan couldn't do it for him. It had to be Richie's decision and his chance to take that last step.

Morgan was about to pull away when Richie's lips met his, gently at first but then deeper, the pressure building. The kiss was as special and tender as the very first they'd shared, and it sent Morgan's heart racing.

Slowly, he climbed on the bed, not wanting to break their lip contact. He slid under the covers next to Richie, chest to chest, their breath mingling as Morgan's hands reacquainted themselves with the delicious curves and lines of Richie's body. "Is this really what you want?"

"Yes. But I don't know if it's what I deserve," Richie said.

"Then it's a good thing that life isn't always fair and that we get things we don't think should come our way." He didn't understand the root of Richie's reticence, though he wished he did. Maybe someday Richie would feel as though he could share it with him. But at the moment, he had much more important things to do, such as see how many of those little groans and whimpers he could pull out of Richie before they both collapsed from sheer satiated exhaustion.

"Are you counting?" Richie asked between gasping breaths a few minutes later after Morgan had rolled him onto his belly and was licking and sucking lightly down his back.

"Of course, sweetheart. You make the best whimpers, and I was seeing how many I could get out of you. I'm up to twenty-three." He rubbed the globes of Richie's ass, parting his cheeks and licking his way toward his tiny opening. "Twenty-four."

Richie chuckled, and Morgan cut it off. There was no need to say twenty-five out loud, or the rest of the numbers between that and forty-two. Richie got the point, and Morgan drove him crazy until he came in a rush of incoherent babbles and then collapsed on the sheet.

"I can't move," Richie whispered. "Give me a minute and I'll...."

"I already came when you did," Morgan whispered.

He got something to clean them up before rejoining him in the bed. They settled with their arms around each other.

"I wish I could believe all of this is true."

"You can do whatever you want to do. It's your belief and within your control. All you need to do is hold on and not let go."

"Like this?" Richie gripped Morgan's arm.

"That's a start," Morgan told him. "Go on and go to sleep." He slid his arm around Richie's waist, where it fit perfectly, and closed his eyes. Exhaustion caught up with him once again, but this time it was mixed with contentment, and sleep came easily and fast. And this time when he woke, there was no disappointment. He was with Richie, holding him in his arms, and that was perfect and felt as it should be. It was perfect... until Richie woke screaming and shaking in his arms.

"I'm here. It's all right," he soothed until Richie's hands reached to Morgan's throat. "Richie," he said and hoped like hell he woke up. Morgan gripped Richie's wrists, pulling his hands away with all the force he could muster. "Richie, you're in bed. It's me, Morgan, and I'm not attacking you." He held him as he thrashed. "Richie, wake up. It's all a dream."

Richie finally opened his eyes and stilled. "Oh my God," he said, looking at each arm where Morgan held him. "What happened?"

"You were having a dream and...."

"I was being attacked, and I fought back." Richie was as pale as a ghost. "Was I…?"

Morgan hesitated to answer. "Yes. I stopped you and woke you up." He released Richie's hands. "What prompted this? You've been quiet for the last few days. At least I haven't heard anything."

"I don't know," Richie said quietly. "I was just sleeping, and then I was back in Iraq on one of my later missions, and we were attacked. I disarmed one of the men, and he came for my neck. I went for his and…." Richie grew even paler. "I strangled him before he could get to me. That's what I thought was happening again."

"It's all right. You were asleep, and you thought you were somewhere else."

"But I could have hurt you or killed you." Richie shook like a leaf.

"Yeah, but you didn't." God, Morgan wanted to know what in the hell had happened to Richie over there. Direct attacks, choking people, being choked…. Everything he learned told him that Richie had gone through complete hell. He took a deep breath and tried to keep from rubbing his throat. He didn't want to draw attention to what had happened or make Richie feel worse.

"Maybe…."

"You should relax and not beat yourself up. It wasn't your fault."

"But what if it happens again?"

"Then maybe you should try to get some help. I know you were at the VA, but I'm talking some specific help for the PTSD. There are support groups that you could go to and talk with other people who are going through the same thing. I know there are things you feel you can't talk about, but what if it's those things that are causing all this for you?"

"It doesn't matter. If it's secret, I can't disclose it. That's the shitty part. It can rip you up inside, but you have to keep it to yourself. When I joined the Corps, I thought the hardest thing would be the physical training and conditioning, but it's not. It's the mental demands. The things that happen to you and the things you can't talk about with anyone, no matter what. They can eat you alive."

Richie leaned closer, and Morgan wrapped him in his arms.

"Sometimes I think I've been eaten away and hollowed out inside until I'm only a shell."

"You're more than that." Morgan closed his eyes, rocking slowly.

Morgan groaned when he heard the alarm bell ringtone from the phone in his bedroom. He would have let it go to voice mail, but it was the station. "Sorry." Morgan hurried and managed to grab the phone before it went to voice mail.

"Ayers. We need you right away. It seems our arsonist struck again. We're going to need all the help we can get."

"I'm on my way." Morgan was already moving through the room to dress as he talked. "Give me ten minutes." He hung up and pulled on underwear and pants. "Richie, I have to go in. There's another fire." He pulled a shirt over his head and hurried to the bed. "I hate to leave like this, but our guy struck again, and I have to get to the scene."

"But it's four in the morning."

"I know, sweetheart. I'll call as soon as I can to let you know that I'm okay, and hopefully I'll be able to leave early." Morgan leaned over the bed. "Go back to sleep, and get some rest." He nuzzled Richie's cheek and then left the room after pulling on shoes and socks.

He barely had time to grab the last of his things before hurrying out of the house and out to his car. "Where is the fire?" Morgan asked as he called in. "I'm in the car on my way."

"It's at 1847 North Third. I sent your gear on truck forty-three, so just meet them there."

"On my way." He drove as fast as he dared and saw the glow of the fire as he approached. Morgan parked out of the way and hurried up to the truck, found his gear and pulled it on.

"Glad you're here," Angus said. "I need you to talk to the families. At least one of them is military, and this really looks like our guy. See if there is anything in common with the other family or your friend. I'd hate to think this guy is just targeting military and ex-military families. I called the fire marshal's office and told them to work through you."

"All right. Is the building under control?"

"Yes, but like the others it's really hot. This looks like a total loss. We're concentrating on keeping it from spreading at the moment."

The captain was called away, and Morgan approached the group of people huddled together. The building was an up-and-down duplex. Many of the residences in this area were.

"I'm sorry," Morgan began. "Did everyone get out safely?"

"Yes," a woman answered. She stood close to her husband, who had the straight and tall bearing of a military man. "Carrie even saved her puppy." The little girl next to them held the squirming puppy for dear life.

"That's excellent. You hold him so he stays safe," he said to her, and she nodded, burying her face in the puppy's fur. "I'm Morgan with the fire department, and I was wondering if you could answer a few questions. Do you know how the fire started?"

"We spoke to the police a little while ago. We smelled gasoline, and then the house just went up. We got everyone out just in time." The man's military toughness sounded about ready to break at any moment. "The people upstairs got out too, but only barely." He looked over at the other small group of people clustered nearby. Then he reached down and lifted the little girl into his arms, his wife taking the puppy, who settled down to sleep in her arms.

"Have you seen anything unusual?"

"No. This is a quiet neighborhood. We all know each other and have a neighborhood watch."

Morgan was willing to bet he was the captain and main organizer.

"Then something like this happens."

"We don't know for sure what's going on," Morgan said.

"I do. I know a fire that was started. I worked in demolition in the army. I know when something has been set on fire, and this definitely was. It smelled like it when we came outside. Why would someone do this?"

"We're not sure. There have been other fires like this, and they seem to be targeting military families." He didn't know what else to tell him. "My home was targeted a few days ago. My roommate is a discharged Marine." He turned when a roar went up, followed by a crash as the upper story collapsed. Hoses centered water on what was left of the house, hissing and sending up a cloud of steam.

"Are you part of any local military organizations?" Morgan asked.

"You don't think—?" He stared as what was left of his home fell in.

"No. I don't think a military person would do this. But I'm trying to figure out how targets are chosen. If we can do that, then maybe we can figure out where he'll try to strike next and catch the bastard."

"I'm a member of the VFW here in Harrisburg," he answered absently. "I take an active role in the organization, but I can't see any of them being involved with something like this."

"If I'm honest, I don't think so either." He turned as a police officer came over. "Antonio," Morgan greeted and shook his hand.

"I'll take over," he said, and Morgan stepped back but stayed close. Antonio asked a lot of questions of both sets of families but learned nothing more than what Morgan had. "The Red Cross is on their way over, and they're going to get you to a motel for the night."

There wasn't a lot to do at this hour but help get these families to shelter for the rest of the night. The fire was largely under control at this point, with what was left of the house quickly burning out, the flames doused by sprays of water.

"Ayers, I think you've done what you can here," the captain said. "Go on and head back to the station and check in. We'll clean up and follow." He clapped Morgan on the shoulder. "Appreciate you coming in to help."

Morgan knew there was nothing else he could do, so he headed back to his car.

He was tired already, and his long shift had just started. Thankfully the station was quiet, and he changed out of his gear and went up to the dormitory, taking an empty bed to get a few hours' sleep. His plans were interrupted an hour later by everyone arriving, and the quiet of the station was turned to a flutter of activity. What was usually a quiet portion of the station was too loud for sleeping, so he gave up and joined the others. It was still too early to call Richie, but he texted him that he was okay and sat at the table and worked his way through multiple cups of coffee so he could wake the hell up.

"Did you find out anything?" the captain asked, sliding into the chair across from him.

"Not much. The owner is former military and a member of the VFW. That doesn't help us because the other fire was just a military family. I need to ask Angus if he did any background on organizations they belonged to, but I don't think Richie is a member of anything at the moment."

"Then there has to be some other connection between them all. I doubt our guy is picking people at random and then burning their houses down."

"I know. But I'm not an investigator, I'm a firefighter. I'll turn the information I have over to Angus. He's much better at this than I am, and he'll keep us in the loop. I agree there is something going on, but I don't know where to go from here."

"All right," he said, lifting his mug. "But I disagree with you. People talk to you during some of the more traumatic times of their lives. They'll open up when they won't with others." He stood. "Talk to your friend Angus, but give that some thought. Getting

others to open up and listening are skills not many people have."
He took his mug with him into the office.

Morgan checked the time and called Richie. "Hey, I'm fine."

"Was the fire bad?"

"Yeah, but no one was hurt."

"So is this guy burning out military families?" Richie asked.

"Yeah."

Richie was silent for a moment. "Have your friends investigate their military backgrounds. Check where everyone was stationed and see if that's the connection. Angus can probably request the information. Tell him to say that military families are being specifically targeted, and that they need help. He needs to make the most of it. It will help part the red tape. Most of the time the military is very insular, but they will go that extra mile for some of their own."

"Thanks. I'll relay the message to him."

"I was going to go to the store today and try to make some dinner. Is there anything you don't like?"

"When it comes to food, I'm pretty easy." He liked the thought of Richie cooking for him. "You don't have to do anything complicated."

"I won't. Be safe, and let me know when you're on your way home."

He liked the way this entire conversation sounded—settled, like they were part of a family. Morgan knew it was way too early and probably delusional to have thoughts like that, but it was how it struck him.

He was more awake after finishing his coffee, so he went down to help the guys with the equipment. He liked to think of being a firefighter as hours of cleaning and preparing their equipment for a few minutes of heart-pounding excitement. If he were honest, he lived for those moments of excitement. That was the best part of the job. By normal shift change, most everything was clean and ready. The night guys went home, and the day shift took over, with Morgan bridging the gap.

"I heard there was another one," Angus said as he strode into the station and over to where Morgan was working.

"Yup. Not much to go on. I hope you guys can find something. One of the residents was former demolitions, and he said the fire was hot and that he smelled gasoline as they were getting out of the building," Morgan relayed. "I'm starting to think this is bigger than Richie. This guy is targeting military families. Richie suggested you investigate military backgrounds for something in common."

"I can try."

"I have an idea as well. This guy keeps doing things the same way. Maybe there's a reason."

"Like revenge for something that happened to him or his family." Angus drummed his fingers on the side of the engine. "That's an interesting thought. But it's going to be like finding a needle in a haystack."

"Maybe. But there have to be records and stories logged somewhere. What if there's an incident somewhere that mimics what's happening here? I'm grasping at straws, but this is so specific. If he was interested in these families in particular, why not change his MO, especially after almost getting caught? There's meaning in it for him."

"I agree. There has to be." Angus pulled out a notepad and began jotting things down. "I'll see what I can find."

"Richie also said that if you contact the military, tell them that military families are being specifically targeted and that their help would keep them safer. I think he was reminding us to appeal to their 'help one of their own' mentality."

"I'll give it a try. We need to catch some sort of break in this case, and right now I feel like we're reacting and spinning our wheels more than we're doing anything else."

He and Angus talked for a little while longer, and then Angus went up to speak with the captain while Morgan went back to work. Thankfully most of the shift was quiet. Morgan kept dreading the next call, hoping it wasn't another of these fires displacing yet another family, or worse. Their only call was for a traffic accident, and thankfully it was only minor injuries.

"RICHIE," HE called, so happy to be home.

"I'm in the kitchen," Richie called back, and Morgan followed his voice.

The house smelled amazing, and Morgan's stomach rumbled at the enticing, earthy aroma.

"Did things get better?"

"Yes, thankfully. Did you get some things done?"

"Yup. I finished a website redesign, and the client was thrilled and they paid me already. I got another job started and made good headway and want to use part of what I got paid to get a new phone. Dinner is in the oven, and I have vegetables on the stove."

"What are you making?"

"Chicken potpie. I made the crusts, and now the pies are in the oven and should be ready in half an hour."

Damn, that smelled good, warm and homey. Morgan nearly tripped over his equipment bag in the laundry room on his way to get the laundry going. When he returned, Richie was checking the oven and then closed the door. Morgan snuck up behind him and leaned over his shoulder.

"This is so wonderful." He kissed him gently and stroked his shoulders. "I appreciate it so much. You have no idea how tired I am of my own cooking and what the guys do at the station. It's all quick food that can wait if we get a call."

"I wanted to do something nice for you."

"You have." Morgan straightened up. "I'll set the table." He got utensils and plates as well as glasses, putting them on the table and then putting down hot pads so Richie would have a place to set his pies.

"I hope you don't get called again."

"Me too." He yawned. "I talked to Angus, and he said he was going to follow your advice. We aren't sure what we're going to get, but this whole thing has me worried. If our arsonist is going after military families, then we need to figure out where he'll strike next, and we can't do that unless we know the reason behind all this." He sat down and held his head. "I'm really getting tired of thinking about this. My captain seems to think I have some particular insight, which I don't, and the others all seem to expect me to have the answers."

"How can you? Unless you're privy to all the information, you can't be expected to solve this particular mystery. I'd say that Angus is the one in the hot seat." Richie opened the oven door and carefully took out the potpies, then placed them on the hot pads on the table.

"Wow, those look really good." His stomach growled louder, and Morgan said a silent prayer that they'd be left alone and that he'd get a chance to eat and rest for a while.

Once Richie was set, Morgan got some water and waited for Richie to pull up to the table before using the hot pads to put a pie on each of their plates.

Steam rose from each of them, carrying the aroma of heaven. Real home cooking was always a treat for him, and dang if it didn't warm his heart that Richie had made this for him. His stomach agreed. He picked up his fork, breaking the crust as more steam rose. It was too hot to eat, yet too good not to get a bite on his fork to cool. "My mother used to make this."

Richie backed away from the table and returned a few seconds later, setting his mother's recipe binder in his hand. "I found it yesterday in the cupboard over there and picked this recipe out of it."

"How did you know which one?"

"This page had the most stains and spatters, so I figured it was one your mother used a lot. If that was the case, it must have been a favorite, so I used it. I can see why. This is wonderfully rich and hearty."

"She used to make it for me and my dad before she died. My dad got rid of most of her things after she died because he couldn't bear to have them around. He was going to throw that away too, but I saved it. I don't know why, because I didn't cook, and you'd think as a kid there would be more important things, but I latched onto it and took it with me wherever my dad and I went."

"Have you cooked out of it?" Richie asked, taking a tentative bite and groaning in delight.

"No."

"Then we need to. The recipes in here are amazing. Just reading them was enough to make me hungry, and this is the only one I got to make." Richie smiled and returned to eating.

Morgan took his first bite and was transported to happier days. He was suddenly a child having dinner at the old round table in their kitchen, his mother putting plates in front of him and Richie at eight or nine. All his childhood memories seemed to include Richie. How could he have forgotten all that?

"I don't know what to say. This is wonderful of you." He ate, and after a few seconds his head felt floaty, as if the lines between past and present had blurred for a few seconds. He was truly transported. He could almost hear the boyish laughter as Richie put his peas on Morgan's plate and in return he gifted Richie with his carrots. Now he ate both carrots and peas, and it seemed Richie did as well, but he wondered how a taste could bring back things he'd forgotten long ago.

"Your mom made this for me too."

"I know."

"Carrots and peas," he said with a smile, and Morgan nodded. "Your mother thought we were hilarious."

"Either that or crazy," Morgan said. "Things changed after she was gone. My dad stopped living and drank too much. I see that now, but at the time I thought he was just sad or something. As I got older I began to understand he was trying to escape and that I wasn't enough for him to stay sober for, at least not for a long time."

"I'm glad this helped you remember your mom."

"And your mom. She stepped in after mine died." Morgan missed both of them very much. "Is it strange to be going down memory lane like this? I used to do it all the time, but it never got me anywhere. I could dream of my mother or being back here with you and your family, but none of it ever came true."

"I used to think that dreams were what made life worth living. That's what my mom used to say. But mine haven't come true lately either, and I stopped dreaming a long time ago. What I want isn't possible to dream to get. My parents are gone, and I will never walk again. Those things are what I want most, and they aren't possible."

"Yeah, well, maybe instead of giving up on dreaming, we need to alter what we wish for." Morgan took another bite and turned his attention to his food. He knew he needed to set his sights in a different direction, and he knew where he wanted them to go, but Richie didn't seem to be particularly interested and was determined to concentrate on what he didn't have as opposed to what was possible. Until he did that, there was little chance for any change.

Their conversation trailed off as they ate. Morgan didn't know what else to talk about, and it seemed that their memories weren't the most welcome of topics.

"It's hard to change what you want when it's all you've been thinking about for a long time," Richie said.

"What is it you really want?" Morgan asked. "Deep in your heart, what do you long for?"

Richie looked at him like he was crazy, but Morgan continued.

"Think about it. You are who you are, just like I am the man I am. There are things within my control and some things that I can't change no matter how much I try. My mother is gone, and nothing will bring her back. So are your parents, and just like them, your ability to walk is gone."

"Aren't you a huge bouquet of flowers," Richie teased.

"In life we sometimes don't like the hand we're dealt. But there are things within our control. And I guess we'd be a lot happier if we concentrated on those." He reached over and stroked a finger along Richie's lightly stubbled jaw. "It doesn't matter to me if you can walk or not. What counts is the person you are."

"Maybe, but what I am isn't a whole person."

Morgan raked his gaze over Richie. "If I were to lose an arm or get burned, would you look at me differently? What if I was to hurt my throat and could no longer speak? Would you look at me the way you seem to look at yourself?"

The house phone rang, the sound jarring and unfamiliar. He'd thought of getting rid of it more than once. Morgan reached over and lifted the receiver.

"Morgan, this is Mrs. Blackwell from across the street."

She was in her seventies and sharp as a tack. Morgan thought she didn't have enough to do, so she watched everything and everyone.

"What can I do for you? Do you need some help?"

"No, honey, but there's someone out in front of your house, and he's been staring at it for the last ten minutes. I know you had some trouble a little while back, so maybe he knows something."

"Thank you." Morgan hung up as his heart beat in his ears. He jumped up, raced to the front door without thinking, and yanked it open just in time to see a figure turn and run off down the street. Morgan thought of going after him, but he had a huge head start, and then a car sped down the street from the direction the man had run, moving like a bat out of hell, so there wasn't much he could do. Morgan tried to get the license plate, but he was too far away and only got a glance at it before the car turned out of sight.

Morgan closed the door and sat back down, then called Angus to tell him what had happened and to relay what information he could about the car.

"He was just watching the house?" Angus asked.

"Yeah. I don't know why, and I wish to hell I could have caught the guy, but he took off jackrabbit fast."

"Okay. I'll check the pictures we have for a car that fits the description and pass the information on to the police. It might help in tracking our boy down."

Morgan's heart rate finally slowed back to something near normal.

"This guy keeps behaving more unpredictably."

"Any luck with the military so far?"

"No. They're holding tight to any information they have. I have access to some very basic information. But it seems that Richie and the other two military victims have one thing in common. They were all in Iraq four years ago outside Baghdad. That could just be a coincidence, because there were plenty of men stationed there, but it's the only thing I've been able to find thus far." Angus sighed. "I'll be in touch if I find anything more solid."

"Thanks." Morgan hung up and tossed his phone on the table in frustration. Whatever was behind this was doing its best to stay hidden.

"Anything?"

"Not much other than you all were in Baghdad at the same time. But that's using a huge net to catch a small fish. There could have been thousands of guys there." Even as Morgan said that he noticed the tension around Richie's eyes. There was something going on, but Morgan was willing to bet that if he asked about it, he'd meet the brick wall of secrecy. "Angus is still looking."

Richie nodded. "I was hoping they'd help, but it looks like he isn't going to get very far."

"I take it you know why," Morgan challenged.

Richie sighed and took another bite of dinner. Morgan figured there was no use in pushing, because Richie wasn't going to talk about it.

"We can't help if we're totally in the dark."

"And I can't tell you," Richie said. "Yeah, I was outside Baghdad for a while, and there were tons of guys there at that time. Mostly we were there as advisors and trainers. The main hostilities had wound down, and we were trying to get the security forces up and running so the last of our forces could go home. That was the goal at that point." Richie set down his fork.

"I could learn that from news reports, but it doesn't tell me why someone is trying to burn all of you out or why some guy was watching the house."

Richie turned to him. His mouth opened and then snapped shut. Richie backed away from the table and began clearing away the dishes. "You and Angus are going to have to look deeper."

"What the hell does that mean?"

Richie slid the dishes onto the counter. "I don't know. There has to be something more to go on than what happened to me over there." Richie turned and wheeled himself out of the room, keeping his back to Morgan. "I wish none of this had ever happened. I was so cocky and sure of myself, going to take on the world." He whirled around. "I've seen things I wished I'd never seen, and every damn night I see it again and again. It's like a bad movie that never fucking comes to an end. It just keeps playing over and over."

"But it may help."

"And it could get me thrown in jail if I tell you something I'm not supposed to. What if I say something and it has nothing to do with what's going on? There are many things about my life that I wish were different, but not being in a military prison isn't one of them. I like my freedom—it's what I fought for, and I don't want it taken away." The agitation in Richie's voice sent shock waves through the room.

"Okay. I know you can't talk about what happened." It was frustrating, because he wanted to help keep them both safe, and he was feeling more and more exposed. Someone had tried to set his house on fire, and now someone was watching the house. This was getting on his nerves more than he wanted to admit. Morgan thought of himself as a strong person, but that was enough to have him jumping at shadows, and he really hated it. "But I'd think you could trust me enough...."

Richie groaned. "This has nothing to do with trusting you."

"Yes, it does. You don't sleep most nights because of what happened, and yeah, I know you were involved in something you can't talk about, but I don't think that's what you're hiding from." God, he hoped he was right. For days Morgan had gotten the idea that there was more to the pain in Richie's eyes than secrecy. Something had happened that had touched Richie's very soul, adding to the darkness and despair that kept showing up.

"Morgan, I can't…." Richie wheeled himself toward the hall.

"Don't, Richie," he said sharply. "Whatever you're so ashamed of, you need to let it go."

Richie wheeled around. "I can't." He looked down at his legs.

"Why? And don't tell me it's secret. Because the wounds on your body and spirit aren't secret at all. They're open for anyone who cares about you enough to see it." And Lord knew he cared about Richie. In his heart he knew Richie was a huge part of his past, but Richie was also his future. That is, if Richie allowed it.

"I can't tell you this," Richie said.

"Am I wrong?" Morgan asked. This was not how he had expected this evening to go. Richie had made a nice dinner, and things had been feeling cozy and warm. Now, with a single phone call, everything had changed. "I'm not accusing you of anything, and I don't want to hurt you. But maybe talking will help you deal with what happened."

"It won't. All it will do is end things." Richie lifted his hard-as-nails gaze. In a few seconds, he looked every bit the unintimidatable Marine.

"Between us, I doubt it," Morgan challenged right back. He wasn't a pushover and could stand his ground. He strode to where Richie sat. "Do you want to build something between us?"

He had to ask, and Richie nodded.

"Then it can't be built on lies and evasion. It needs to be built on trust and honesty." Morgan turned away and went back to the table, where he cleared the last of the dishes. He cleaned the table and kept working. Morgan knew he'd just delivered an ultimatum, and he half expected Richie to run. But he had to know what had been eating at Richie so badly.

He rinsed all the dishes and then loaded them in the dishwasher, purposely not turning around. Morgan moved rhythmically, adding the plates and glasses to the others. Once it was loaded, he closed the door and started the machine. Fatigue and lack of sleep were catching up with him, and his ability to think clearly was becoming compromised. He stood at the sink, gripping the edge of the counter as frustration built. "Can't you fucking see that I want to help you?" Morgan growled.

"You've done enough of that," Richie finally answered.

"Not possible." He wanted to rip the counter off the cupboards. This cat and mouse shit was driving him crazy. "If you don't want my help, then I can live with that. I can also live with you not caring enough about me or yourself to do something about what's getting deep into your soul, but I can't...." He continued looking away. "I can't be involved with you... in that way."

"So if I don't talk then we can't be together?"

"Yes." He inhaled and released it slowly. "I dealt with a father to whom alcohol was more important than I was for a long time. Whatever it is that you're hiding, you can hold it deep if you want, but I won't let someone put something like that in front of me again. I support and care for my friends, but I can't live like that, not with a lover, someone I'd like to be with for a long time. That's more than I can deal with."

"So what do you want from me?"

Morgan stared at the sink. "I want you to decide what's important to your life, if it's the secrets that will eat you alive from the inside, over me. My dad's drinking ate him away, and this will do the same thing to you." Morgan finally lifted his gaze and then turned around. "I want to thank you for the dinner. It was really nice." He felt defeated and hollow. Morgan had really thought there was something between them, but maybe Richie had been right. He must have wanted things to work between them so badly that he deluded himself. "Just think about it." He had to leave the door open somehow.

"Do you know what you're asking?" Richie questioned. "I've tried to forget this and go on with my life, and you want me to talk about the deepest wound I've ever had."

"Who else can you talk to but your oldest friend? Who's known you at your best and worst?"

"We were thirteen. Our best and worst then was sneaking the candy from my mom's cupboard. We hadn't lived. I've seen more of the worst side of life than I ever thought was possible, and you think you know me?" Richie pounded his hands on the arms of the chair.

"Yeah, I know you. I know you have a good heart and that when you laugh your eyes twinkle and you forget about what happened to you for just a few minutes and the thirteen-year-old I knew comes out. I know that whatever it is you're hiding is tearing you up, because you never kept secrets, not from me."

"Things change."

"Yes, they do, but you're still that same person. You took care of me back then. I know it was you and your mom who made sure there were a few presents for me under the tree. They certainly weren't from my dad."

Richie's gaze faltered. "Damn it."

"You can't hide. Time may have separated us, but you can't run away from the person you are."

"This is me." Richie put his hands out. "That's all there is. A guy in a chair."

"Oh, give up that crap. You're more than the chair, and you know it. So man up and stop taking the easy way out. I know that's what they told you in the Corps when things got tough. You either man up or wash out. And I know you never washed out of anything in your life. So don't start now." Morgan could see that his words hurt, but he knew he was right. "You can do anything, chair be damned. You just have to want it bad enough. So what do you want?" Morgan asked for the third time. "You never answer the question. You'll talk about how hard things are or anything else, but you never answer the question that's at the heart of the matter. When you do, everything will be clear, and you won't have to worry about things so much."

"How do you know this?"

"Because I had to decide what I wanted. Did I want a father who loved alcohol more than me? When I answered that question, the rest was easy. I could go my own way and find my own path without his drinking and his behavior like a millstone around my neck." Morgan stepped closer. "Let me ask you this. Knowing what you do now and the man you are, would you do anything differently?"

"You mean would I still join the Corps?" Richie asked.

Morgan nodded.

"Yeah, I think I would."

"Then there's your answer." Could it possibly have been that easy? "If you wouldn't change anything, then the outcome would be the same. And in the end you'd be the person you are right now, dealing with PTSD and everything else that happened. So why fight it?"

Richie's mouth opened and closed like a fish. "I…."

"You never thought about it that way. But everything that happens to us makes us the person we are. None of us gets to pick and choose. I certainly didn't, and neither did you. So what's it going to be, accept who you are, let go of the crap, and allow yourself to be happy, or hold everything inside until it eats you alive? The choices aren't all that difficult."

"You know, sometimes you're a real know-it-all pain in the ass." A touch of mirth shone in Richie's eyes.

"I've been told that once or twice. I take it as a compliment."

Richie rolled closer. "You look about ready to drop. Can you and I talk tomorrow? You need to get to bed because they're going to want you early in the morning."

Morgan nodded and went down the hallway to his bedroom. He had no real idea where this left them, and he was way too tired to ask or try to find out. His legs felt like they were made of lead, and his bed was singing a siren song.

Chapter 6

RICHARD STAYED where he was, watching Morgan's incredible backside retreat down the hallway. He wasn't sure what to do, so he rolled through the room turning out the lights and sat in the dark. He needed time to think. He'd promised to speak with Morgan tomorrow, but he wasn't sure if he could actually go through with it. Maybe he should have blurted out the whole thing to get it over with.

He picked up his phone to check the time and scrolled through the contacts that had been stored and could be brought down to his new phone. There weren't many. He found the one he wanted and stared at the number. Then he pressed the button and listened for the ring.

"Hello," the familiar voice said tentatively.

"Snoop, its Smalley."

"Well, I'll be damned. I thought you'd fallen off the face of the earth. How in the hell are you?" He sounded really happy, and children's high-pitched voices called out from behind him.

"As well as can be expected, I guess."

"Did things work out for you?" Snoop asked.

"Depends. I'm alive but in a chair." He'd stayed away from the other men in his unit. After what had happened, he hadn't been able to face any of them. "I will be for the rest of my life."

"Because of what happened?" Snoop asked.

"Yeah. I guess I got what I deserved." The words slipped out before he could stop them.

"What the… heck are you talking about? Yeah sh… stuff went south fast, but that wasn't your fault. We had bad intelligence. Really bad."

"I was the one in charge, and I should…."

"Is that why you disappeared? We were told there was a small group hiding out, not nearly a hundred men." Snoop seemed to be willing to overlook what happened, but Richard couldn't. His brothers, men he'd known and grown to care for, were dead because of him, and nothing anyone said could change that. He should have been more cautious and made sure the intelligence was right.

"Yeah," Richard finally answered. He was grateful Snoop didn't press him for more.

"So why the call after all this time? Not that it isn't good to hear from you, though."

Once again his voice was bright, and it buoyed Richard's mood.

"Have you told anyone what happened?"

"Christy knows. I told her what happened and what we went through. She's put up with flashbacks and God knows what else. But I've worked through a lot of it, and the attacks happen a lot less often. I take it you haven't told anyone."

"No. It was secret."

"Yes, it was. I gave no details, but she deserved to know some of what I went through. How else can she help? And how could I get it off my chest so I could start to heal? The whole thing was eating me alive. Nothing is worth your soul, certainly not some mission in a war that should never have happened. Talk to someone close, and see if it doesn't give you some peace. After what we've been through, we all deserve it." He was so sincere.

"From what I hear behind you, things have really changed for you."

"They have. I have two girls that I live for, and I'm not nearly the SOB I was a few years ago." He covered the phone, and when he returned the noise was much less. "I was terrible when I was discharged. I kept thinking the world should work the way the military did."

"Yeah. Nothing does. Although I spent months in the hospital, so there was plenty of hurry up and wait."

"I'm sure there was, and it's the shits that you had to go through that. I heard Franklin is in some sort of rehab. He stayed in and was injured three months after you left. It was pretty bad, but I hear he's getting better."

Thankfully Snoop didn't talk about the guys who didn't make it home. Richard didn't think he could take that right now.

"It's good he's getting better," Richard said.

"It is. He had three little ones, and they're having a tough time of it, though."

They talked about some of the other guys in the unit. A few were getting married, one divorced. What was conspicuous for Richard were all the guys they would no longer talk about because they were gone.

"I need to let you go. It's time to get the girls into bed, and I have to read them their stories before they go to sleep. Man, let me tell you, there is nothing so wonderful as having a family and kids of my own."

"It sure sounds good on you."

"You should get one."

"I need to get my head screwed on straight first."

"Then if you don't mind my asking, what prompted the call? I expected you were asking because you had someone you wanted to open up to. Is there a woman you're interested in?"

Now was the moment of truth. "Not a woman, no. A guy. We were friends together as kids, and now I think we're working on being more, but he says I need to be honest and open." Richard had no idea what kind of reaction to expect from his Marine brother.

Initially the line went really quiet. "Relationships always start with honesty. If you're hiding things, the relationship rots from the inside."

It seemed the whole gay thing was no big deal.

"When did you get to be such an expert?" Richard teased.

"I guess I got really lucky." Contentment flowed through the phone like a balm. "Tell the guy in your life whatever you need to. Get it off your chest, and then put it behind you and get on with living. We all saw too much and did things we never would have done anywhere else. But you're home now, so build one where you can feel safe."

"Daddy," Richard heard on the line in the background, and he smiled to himself.

"Thank you," he told Snoop.

"Call anytime. It was great to hear from you, and if you're ever in Chicago, you need to stop in for a visit. We'd love to see you."

He said good-bye, and Richard ended the call.

He shuffled to put his phone back in his pocket and then stared out the front window. Everyone seemed to be telling him the same thing, and yet he was still too nervous to talk about it. But he'd promised, and it was too late to take that back now. He was a man of his word, and he wasn't going to break it.

Richard slowly turned away and wheeled down the hall to the bathroom. He cleaned up and returned to the hallway, looking at the open door to Morgan's room. Richard rolled closer and then turned around again.

"Richie," he heard Morgan say softly, and he entered the dark bedroom, wheeling over to the bed. He heard Morgan shift, and the covers lifted in invitation.

Richard wished there was an elegant way for him to get into bed, but there wasn't. He lifted himself and managed to make it onto the mattress without falling on his ass. Then the covers fell over him, and he was encased in a cocoon of warmth.

"Go to sleep. We'll talk in the morning, and whatever it is that you've been hiding, I can almost guarantee it will be worse in your mind than it will be in real life." Morgan rolled onto his side and held him, tugging Richard until they pressed close together.

"I thought you were sleepy," Richard teased as Morgan's long, hard erection pressed to his hip, which sent Richard's mind in an amorous direction.

"Certain parts don't seem to want to listen."

Morgan rolled him onto his back and then leaned over him, pressing their lips together in a kiss that nearly stopped Richard's heart. They made love—at least that's how Richard would always remember it—slowly and carefully, with Morgan taking plenty of time. Richard was still nervous about what Morgan was going to think of him after he told him what happened, but he put that aside. He had decided to be honest with him and to let the chips fall where they may. That gave him a certain freedom, and Richard pulled Morgan close and rolled onto his side with Morgan behind him.

The preparations were mind-blowingly slow, with Richard half begging Morgan to move faster. "I want to feel you."

"You will. But I won't hurt you, and I want this to be special." Morgan used fingers and even his tongue to drive him wild. Richard stroked himself damn near to the edge and backed off. He wanted Morgan inside him. It had been so very long since he felt alive, and regardless of what happened, he wanted to be with Morgan once.

A single tear rolled down Richard's cheek, falling onto the pillow as Morgan held him tight and slowly entered him. "Jesus, God," he breathed as the stretch and intimacy nearly overwhelmed him.

"Is that good or bad?" Morgan asked, stopping.

Richard grunted and pressed back, not wanting Morgan to stop.

"Good, then?"

"Hell yes." His mind cleared, and all the doubt and angst flew away like a bird, and Richard hoped it wasn't a homing pigeon, because he never wanted to feel like that again. He wanted what he had right now, his heart racing, sweat beading on his skin as he was truly alive. "Don't you dare stop!"

"I won't," Morgan hissed in his ear as he pressed, hips to butt, holding still, cock buried inside him.

Damn, that felt good, filling. The connection between the two of them better than any of the drugs he'd been given after his injury. There had been so many times when he'd waited for those painkillers, praying they'd make him fly pain free for a few hours. This was better than that. Everything was heightened, the throb inside him, the stretch and pull, Morgan's hand on his belly steadying him. The way his lips touched his shoulder at first, followed by the light scrape of teeth that sent a ripple running down his back.

"I need this, needed you."

"So do I," Morgan admitted, sending Richard into overload.

"I wish I knew the hell why," Richard said, and Morgan slammed into him, stealing the air from his lungs.

"We are not going there again," Morgan groaned and sped up. "We've already had that conversation, and it's over." He pulled away and punctuated his point with a thrust that reverberated to Richard's toes. "Some things you have to take on faith, and let me tell you, I'll slip you my faith over and over until you fucking feel it well into next week."

Richard's eyes rolled into his head as Morgan did just that. "I thought you were tired," he teased between gasps.

"I'll show you who's tired," Morgan challenged and quickened his pace. "I'll make love to you all night and well into the dawn if that's what it takes to get my point across. Stop questioning and start believing this can be real if you want it badly enough."

"I do," Richard moaned, grabbing the bedding and holding on for dear life. He wished he could see Morgan, but this position was comfortable, so he turned his head as far as he could, and Morgan reached his lips, kissing him as if he was passion and heat personified.

"Then act like it and hold on to what you want."

Richard grabbed Morgan's hand and threaded their fingers together. As Morgan drove their passion, he tightened his grip, not wanting to let Morgan go. He wanted to believe he finally had someone who would care for him and put him first. Richard wanted to believe he could be loved as he was and could stop feeling like a failure and incomplete. "You are everything."

"You're even more," Morgan whispered before sucking on his ear. Richard rested his head back against Morgan, closed his eyes, and let the waves of delight wash over him.

"Damn," he moaned softly. That was a lot headier than he expected, and as Morgan's movements became erratic and his own almost wild and frantic, he held on as the tingling began at the base of his spine, fanned out, and bloomed into a release that left him floating and happier than he could remember being in a very long time.

Richard didn't want to move. Everything was perfect at the moment, and he knew things rarely stayed that way for more than a few seconds. The world and reality had ways of invading that happened in the form of a cramp in his hip. He shifted slightly, and that was enough for him and Morgan to separate. "I need to get a cloth for you," Morgan said softly and kissed his shoulder before leaving the bed. A cool draft drifted up Richard's backside. Thankfully Morgan was quick, and he returned and replaced the cool air with warmth, cleaning him up and then putting the cloth away. When Morgan settled once again, Richard got comfortable and drifted off to sleep.

When he woke again, it was still dark, and Morgan was getting back into bed. "What's wrong?"

"I thought I heard something," Morgan explained as he pulled the covers up. "Go back to sleep. It was nothing."

"You have to do something about this." Richard groaned, wanting to go back to sleep. "You can't be up two or three times a night because you're worried that guy will come back. If you want to be able to work, you need rest."

"I know." Morgan rolled over. "I was thinking about what Angus said and about getting a dog, but I need help taking care of it. I work weird hours and…."

"Like Mitzy?" he interrupted, really liking that idea.

"Yeah, something like that."

Morgan yawned, and Richard grew quiet. He found it comforting that Morgan wanted to get a dog and had asked him to help, like he was going to be around for a while. Richard had always felt this was a temporary arrangement. Hell, he half expected Morgan to tell him to leave at any time.

"Stop thinking whatever you're thinking," Morgan whispered, already half asleep. "I can hear those wheels turning."

"I know."

"You're a Marine, and you can handle anything that life throws at you."

Morgan grew quiet, and light snores told Richard he was asleep already. Richard dug into his Marine training and turned off the churning wheels in his mind and went to sleep as well.

RICHARD WORKED hard the following day. He made sure Morgan got something to eat before he left and then settled at the kitchen table with the laptop Morgan had loaned him and got to work. He stopped for lunch and then continued working all afternoon until his neck, back, and arms ached a little. Richard was driven, and he needed something to keep his mind off the conversation he'd promised Morgan they were going to have.

He kept checking the clock and kept his phone nearby. Morgan usually called if he was going to be late, and it was getting to the time when he'd usually be home. Richard turned on the television news, but they were no help, so he checked the Internet for any stories about fires in the area. But there were none. He was about to call Morgan when his phone rang. Richard snatched it up and did his best to remain calm when the number displayed wasn't familiar.

"Richie, it's Kevin. I got a call from Angus. They've been called to a huge fire on the east side. Apparently it's in one of the townships, and they have put out the alert for all possible responders."

"I checked the news...."

"This hasn't hit yet, but he said it's a huge one. Do you want me to come over? I hate sitting alone and worrying at times like this. I usually spend them with the guys, but they all went to Disney for the week with their husbands. Angus couldn't get off work, and I didn't want to be a third wheel."

"Then come on over, and we'll wait together. And bring Mitzy," Richard said with a smile.

"I will."

Kevin hung up, and Richard made some lemonade. By the time he was done, he called for Kevin to come in at the knock on the door, and Mitzy raced to him.

"Hey, girl," Kevin scolded and took the tray with the pitcher and glasses as Mitzy tried to jump into Richard's lap. "She gets excited when she sees someone she likes."

"Let's go into the living room." Richard gave up trying to move until Kevin led the way and Mitzy followed him, her golden tail wagging. Then he rolled in and got out of his chair and into Morgan's favorite one. He loved this chair. It was perfectly comfortable, and it smelled like Morgan. "So what usually happens at times like these?"

"We usually sit around, eat junk food, watch the news, and worry our fingers to the bone. The guys come over, and we play video games. I create them, and they test them out for me. I did one for fire department training."

"That's right. I remember. Morgan said he was going to bring me in so I could see it, but he hasn't had a chance." He found the remote and turned on the news once again. This time the lead story was a huge fire in Paxton Township. The newscaster was standing down the road, and even from that distance, flames could be seen leaping in the background.

"The old Westland Inn sat empty for years, and now it's going up in flames," the newscaster began dramatically. "The inn had no guests, but we're told there were caretakers on the property who were initially unaccounted for."

He went on to explain what happened, and Richard wished they would pan closer so he could get a better look at the firefighters. He wanted to see that Morgan was all right.

There were no closer pictures, and as he watched, a fireball went up in the background.

"What the hell was that?" Kevin asked as the newscaster pretty much asked the same question, with better language.

"We'll be investigating as soon as we can, but we are all being kept away for safety."

He went on to explain about the hotel and all, but Richard barely heard him.

"They send Morgan inside. That was how he saved me," Richard said.

"Angus is an active kind of guy too. He saved me from a fire once." Kevin smiled, and Mitzy jumped up next to him, settling with her head in his lap. "We have that in common, I guess."

"Yeah," Richard agreed as he continued watching the television. They had gone on to another story but promised to return before the end of the broadcast. "How in the heck can you do this?" His heart pounded as he tried not to think of what could be happening to Morgan at this moment.

"It's part of caring for them. Being a firefighter is as much a part of their lives as breathing. They couldn't do anything else if they tried."

"But what if they don't come home?"

Kevin nodded slowly, continually stroking Mitzy's head, her eyes drifting shut and then opening again. "Angus said you were a Marine. It's the same thing. They have their job. It's dangerous, and it keeps other people safe. They also live and breathe it, just like I'm sure you did when you were in the Corps."

"Yeah, I suppose."

"Firefighters also take care of each other."

This was starting to sound very familiar. He'd never really thought Morgan could understand the life he'd led. He hadn't thought that he was still living it, just in a different form. "I can understand that."

"And there are crap times like this when we sit at home and worry the hell over them because they're at a fire that we know is dangerous and we want them to come back safe. That was part of the reason Angus got us Mitzy, so I wouldn't be alone when times get sucky like this."

"How do you do it, though?"

"I man up and know that I have to be strong for Angus. If he knew I sat at home and was worried as hell and didn't want him to be out there in harm's way, he'd be thinking of me rather than doing his job, and that would put him in more danger. So I do my best to go on and support him."

"Does he know you're here?"

"Nope. And when he calls I'll tell him you and I were watching television and talking about dogs or something. If I was with the guys I'd say we'd decided to have a video game night or something, and when Angus got home, he'd find us all crowded together in front of the television, playing games." Kevin bit his lower lip. "Usually I'm able to hide the fact that the television is also tuned to the news so we can find out if anything happened."

"So you're basically like me, worried sick with nothing you can do about it." Richard sighed and turned back to the television.

"Basically, yeah," Kevin answered. "But Angus is worth it. I'll worry over him any number of nights because he's worth worrying over."

Richard squirmed slightly under Kevin's intense gaze.

"Besides, if something bad happened to Angus, I'd know it."

"How?"

"I can feel him inside me all the time. He's firmly lodged in my heart, and the last time he got hurt, I just knew. It was a feeling, like a tremble that went up my back and stayed in my gut. It didn't go away. Tristan said it was gas, but I knew something had happened to Angus. He got burned and they took him to the hospital, but he was fine and needed some time to recover."

"Do you really think you'd know if he was hurt?" Richard asked, hoping he and Morgan developed that mind connection.

"I don't know. It could have been gas like Tristan said, but I like to think that I'd know if something happened to Angus, and I'm pretty sure by the way you look at each other that there's a deep connection between you and Morgan."

Richard tilted his head slightly. "I've known him just a few weeks."

"No. You were childhood friends, and Morgan watches you like you set the stars in motion and they all center on you." Kevin scooted to the edge of the sofa, and Mitzy raised her head, blinked a few times, and then settled once more. "Do you ever know where Morgan is even though you shouldn't? Say he's coming up behind you and you didn't hear him, but you know he's there and expect his touch before it actually happens?"

"Yeah, but…."

"I could come up on you from behind and startle you. But Morgan can't because you know he's there."

"I guess so. I never tested it, but I know where he is and what he's doing most of the time when he's home."

Kevin nodded. "See, you have that connection to him."

"But that's just coincidence." He wasn't sure he believed what he thought Kevin was trying to tell him. "Is this some kind of soul-mate thing? That's just a romantic notion."

"I don't think so. There are stories all the time of people being together for fifty years and then dying within days of each other. Their lives and energy were so entwined that they couldn't exist without the other person. I believe they were soul mates, and it's possible you have that with Morgan."

Richard was finding this hard to believe. "We were friends years ago and share a history."

"Maybe. But how many old friends take them in after a fire when they haven't seen each other in twenty years? How many old friends build ramps onto their home? I think it's possible that

Morgan feels the connection already, and you haven't opened yourself up to it."

Kevin was so insistent that Richard decided not to argue.

"Let me tell you this. You say you've only really known him for a few weeks. If that's true and you and Morgan are just casual friends who sleep together, then why are you wound up so tight your hand shakes when you don't have it resting on the arm of the chair?" Kevin cocked his eyebrow and nodded once in a "so there" kind of way.

"If this is true, then what do I do?" Richard asked, humoring Kevin more than anything else.

"Just open yourself to the possibility. Morgan came to your aid and has stayed there since he found you."

Richard turned his attention to the television, which was running commercials. "Did Morgan tell you that he and I were married?" Richard grinned at the shock on Kevin's face. "We were thirteen, and our friend Amy insisted on it."

"So the two of you agreed to marry each other? You know boys don't do that. Heck, I'm as gay as they come, and that would have freaked me out at thirteen."

"Amy said we could ride ponies, and we were waiting for her mother," Richard explained, even as he wondered if what Kevin said was true. "The thing is that Morgan kept the ring. It was a nail bent round into a circle, but he still had it."

"So something from when he was thirteen meant enough to him that he kept that piece of iron all those years? Can't there be something more to it than him being sentimental?"

"I don't know," Richard answered honestly. "We were thirteen at the time, kids who didn't know anything other than that we were different."

"Did you know you were gay even then?"

"I think so. I didn't have the words, but I talked to Morgan about it, and he told me right back. We were clumsy and awkward, but we believed each other, and once Morgan moved away, at least I knew there was one other person in the world like me." He turned back to the television, where the same reporter was framed in the screen.

"We've just received word that the fire that has been blazing at the Westland Inn seems to be burning itself out. Apparently the empty hotel was being used for storage, and that complicated the efforts of firefighters." He turned toward the fire. "We have seen ambulances heading toward the fire scene, but we're being kept away. We'll stay on the scene and bring you updates as they become available."

He signed off, and Richard turned to Kevin.

"They wouldn't bring in ambulances for nothing."

"Yes, that's true. But we can't jump to conclusions. Someone could have been injured, and they brought them in for first aid and to look them over. You never know."

"How can you be so logical?" Richard asked.

"Because I've been through this before. There's no sense worrying about things we don't know." Kevin poured glasses of the lemonade and handed one to Richard. "You need something to take your mind off it." Kevin took his phone out of his pocket and put it on the coffee table. "They'll call as soon as they can."

Richard honestly wasn't sure why he was freaking out. He'd been through much worse than a hotel fire. "I saw some really bad fires when I was in Iraq. Some of our guys had taken refuge in a damaged office building. One of the militias set the building on fire to try to smoke them out. Thankfully we were able to fight off the militia members for long enough that the other Marines were able to get out. Then we let it burn and got the hell away. The place went up like a Roman candle."

"You've seen heavy combat?" Kevin asked. Richard nodded. "How did you keep your cool?"

"The adrenaline was flowing, and we were trained to behave a specific way. When push comes to shove, you react, which is why our training was so intense, to make sure we react the right way. It's only afterwards that I thought about what could have happened to me. It's not like this, where we sit and wait without being able to do anything about it."

"Everything will be fine. I know it sucks to be sitting and waiting."

Mitzy jumped down off the sofa and walked to Richard's chair, then placed her head in his lap, looking at him with doleful eyes. Richard stroked her head.

"I know. You're worried about your daddy too."

"She's very intuitive, and I've been thinking of having her trained as a therapy dog. She loves people and seems to understand when we're hurting or nervous."

"She'd be good at that," Richard said, looking into her big brown eyes. "You're such a good girl."

Richard jumped when Kevin's phone rang. Mitzy pulled away and loped back over to Kevin.

"It's Angus," he said with a smile and then answered the phone. "Are you all right?" Kevin asked right away and then smiled. "I didn't think you were hurt. What about Morgan and everyone else?"

Kevin listened, and Richard watched him for any sign of bad news.

"Thanks, I'm here with him and will let him know." Kevin hung up. "The fire is still burning. Angus said that two firefighters were injured, neither severely. Morgan is fine, but one of the men from his station was hurt, and he's going with him to the hospital. Angus said Morgan will call when he can."

"So he's fine?"

"Yeah, but apparently one of the younger men from the station didn't fare so well."

"Okay. At least he's fine." Richard liked that Morgan was helping his fellow firefighter. It was what he would do for one of his Marine brothers.

"Angus said the man who was hurt was one of the guys that Morgan worked with a lot and that Morgan had been mentoring Henry and trying to help show him the ropes. Angus didn't have the details of how he got hurt, but Angus said the guys were saying that Morgan pulled him out of the building just in time."

"That seems to happen a lot with Morgan." From what he'd been told, that's what Morgan had done for him as well. "I keep wondering if Morgan takes unnecessary risks."

"That coming from a Marine. Aren't you guys like the super soldiers or something?" Kevin grinned and answered his phone when it rang again. "Yeah, he's there and fine." Kevin laughed. "Go have your picture taken with Mickey." He chuckled once again and hung up. "Zach saw a story on his phone about the fire, and he wanted to make sure Angus was all right."

He used to have friends like that when he was in the Corps, but now they were scattered to the winds. After calling Snoop, he knew he needed to be the one to reach out and try to rebuild some of those old ties. No one could understand what he'd been through better than they. Maybe more of them felt the way Snoop did. Guilt was a strange thing.

When his phone rang, he snatched it off the table next to him. "You better be okay, because if you're not I'm going to kill you." The waiting had most definitely gotten to him.

"I'm fine," Morgan said. "I'm at the hospital now. Henry was pouring water on the fire, and he was too close when one of the walls collapsed. I got to him and was able to get him out, but not before he got burned. Hopefully it isn't too bad. They're looking at him now."

"Angus called Kevin, and he brought Mitzy over. We've been keeping each other company. He said you were okay, but it's so good to hear your voice. Take care of Henry, and come home as soon as you can."

"I will."

He heard the longing in Morgan's voice and turned away because that seemed too private even to share his reaction with someone else.

"Then be safe, and let me know if there's anything we can do for Henry."

"They've called his family, and his mother is on her way up. Once he isn't alone, I'll come home."

Morgan said a quiet good-bye and hung up. Richard set the phone back on the table.

"He's fine. I'm so happy you came over with Mitzy."

Hearing her name, she came back over for some attention.

"Morgan was interested in getting a dog, and he asked if I'd help care for him."

"I think that's great," Kevin said as Richard's phone pinged. He checked the message.

"Could you bring me my laptop?" A client was asking for some information, and he wanted to send it right away. "It's just over on the table." He'd get it himself, but that would mean a whole lot of shifting. Kevin was nice enough to jump up and bring it to him.

"Did it survive the fire?"

"Morgan had an extra, and he loaned it to me." Richard logged in and retrieved the information he needed, then sent it to the client. A few minutes later, his phone dinged, saying he'd just been paid. That was a great feeling, having some money of his own in his account. He made a note to talk to Morgan about how he could help out for staying here. He closed the lid and left the laptop resting on his legs.

Richard changed the channel until he found one Kevin seemed to like. Then he rested back in the chair, drank his lemonade, and spent a quiet hour or so with his new friend until Mitzy perked up and then raced to the back door, growling deep in her throat.

"There's no one in the driveway," Kevin said before hurrying to the back door.

By then Mitzy was barking her head off, and Richard heard her clawing at the door. Kevin must have opened it because he heard her barking from outside and across the lawn. Richard was able to turn and push aside the curtains enough to see a man running off down the street. Mitzy stopped at the edge of the grass, barking loudly until Kevin called her back.

"Some guy was around the side of the house," Kevin said as Mitzy hurried back into the living room. She settled next to his chair, and the back door smacked closed. Richard waited a few minutes until Kevin came back inside.

"Did you see anything?" Richard asked.

"No. But I'll take Morgan out when he comes home, and he can look." Kevin sank back into the sofa, and when Mitzy came over he praised her effusively. "You scared away the burglars, didn't you?"

"I swear if she'd have gotten hold of him…."

"She'd probably have peed and then rolled over. She's all bark and no bite, but he didn't know that." He continued stroking her head. Kevin's phone rang again, and he answered it and then got ready to go. "That was Angus. He said he was on his way home, so I'm going to take her highness here and get out of your hair. You have my number, so if you need anything, just call." Kevin hurried over and gave him a warm hug.

"Thanks for everything," Richard called and began shifting back to his wheelchair.

"Don't get up. I'll let myself out, and be sure to tell Morgan about our visitor. I'm not sure what he was doing here."

"I will." Richard waved good-bye, and once he got to his chair, he rolled to the front door to watch him go.

The house seemed empty and too dang quiet. Once he shut the door, Richard turned up the television for company and then went to the kitchen to start some dinner.

MORGAN DRAGGED in an hour later looking even more tired than he had the night before.

"Thank God that's over and I have a few days off." He dropped his bag in the laundry room and sat in one of the kitchen chairs.

"Dinner will be ready in half an hour. Why don't you go ahead and shower, because you smell like fire, and by the time you're done, we'll be ready to eat."

Richard tilted his head upward, and Morgan leaned down for a kiss. Richard shared the deep kiss and used the chance to cop a feel of Morgan's firm backside. Damn, he felt good.

"If you keep doing that, we'll end up going right to dessert."

Richard pulled away. "You're too tired and hungry for that. So go shower, and we'll definitely have dessert later." He flashed Morgan a smile and made sure to have the food on the table by the time Morgan came back out, his hair still wet. Richard loved that look on him, no cares, and at least for a few seconds he looked like the boy he remembered from all those years ago.

"Sit down, and I'll be right over."

"Pot roast," Morgan said, sitting down with a grin. "I haven't had that since…." He stopped. "Is that from my mother's recipes?"

"Yes." Richard was so pleased he seemed to have made Morgan happy. "Was the fire as bad as Angus told Kevin?"

"It was pretty bad. Henry, the firefighter who was injured, is going to be fine. He got burned, but I was able to get to him in time, and it wasn't as bad as it could have been. His arm will be sore for a while and he'll need to rest and check for infection, but it could have been a lot worse." Morgan tucked in enthusiastically.

"Before I forget. Mitzy about had a fit, and she chased someone away from the side of the house. Kevin didn't see anything, but you might want to check just to be safe." Richard began eating rather slowly as thoughts of what he'd promised crept back into his mind. He knew he'd put it off as long as he dared, and now that he'd had a chance to really think it over, trying to put his own fear aside, he knew Morgan should know.

"It was my last assignment. I had decided that I was going to make the Marines my career and figured in a few months I'd sign up for the long haul."

Morgan looked up from his plate and thankfully didn't say anything.

"You probably heard that there were, and are, a huge number of factions in Iraq, which is what no one counted on when we started this mess after 9/11. They had been repressed for a long time but came roaring back once the regime was out of power."

"I remember them talking about it on the news at one point. It was all pretty hard to follow with the ten-second sound bites we got," Morgan explained as he continued eating.

Richard wondered if he should have waited until after they'd finished eating, but he'd started, and there was no going back now. "We were very close to clearing this particular area of Baghdad and pulling it from under the influence of a particularly nasty warlord. Intelligence told us that he'd gathered the last of his men and had transported them out of the city and that they were holed up in a series of underground passages. It was our job to flush them out and put an end to this group once and for all. The people they were supposed to represent had turned on them, and their support had waned." He took a bite but found his appetite had taken wing.

Morgan set down his fork, turning toward him. "What happened?"

"I should have verified the information we were given," Richard said right away.

"Just tell me what happened," Morgan said.

"We put together a team to flush out these men, about fifty men. It should have been more than enough. We were experts at getting in and out of places most people would find impossible. We planned, trained, and then deployed."

Morgan's gaze didn't shift. "You said the intelligence was wrong and that you should have checked it."

Richard nodded. "This was supposed to be a routine maneuver, and I was given the lead for the first time."

"What went wrong?"

"There were supposed to be thirty men holed up. It turned out there were over a hundred and fifty. He'd been recruiting, and his numbers had swelled. Saddhar put out the word that he was in trouble, and he smuggled in men and material. They were waiting for us, and they let us get into position before opening fire with more force than we could counter. I called for help, but it was too late. They were already cutting us to ribbons. Twenty men were killed or wounded before air strikes sent the enemy scattering."

"You were one of the injured," Morgan said.

Richard nodded. "They said I was lucky because they could save my legs, but I wouldn't be able to use them. There is just enough of my spinal cord left unsevered for me to feel my legs, but that's all. The rest is gone and isn't coming back. Neither are the men who lost their lives because I didn't double-check that the intelligence was right."

"Who gave it to you?"

"My commander, but that's still no excuse. If I'd have looked and dug deeper, we could have found the information we needed. Instead I went in with what I was given, and ten men went out in body bags and others with various wounds and injuries, all because of me." Richard pushed back from the table. "That's what I see almost every night in my dreams. The men in my unit being mowed down and incinerated because of something I didn't do."

"Your commander was the one who fed you bad information. Did he stand up for you?"

"No. He tried to weasel out of it."

"Was there an investigation?" Morgan asked, leaning a little closer.

"Yeah. In the end the court-martial found him guilty, and they chose not to charge me, but that doesn't matter. I had the power to do things better, and I didn't. Anyway, after it became apparent that I would never walk again, they discharged me, and I went into a hospital and rehab facility."

"And you've been blaming yourself for what happened ever since."

"I am to blame. Doesn't matter what the Corps or anyone says—I know I'm to blame for that." He had to try to make Morgan understand.

"Wait… you said incinerated. What did you mean by that?"

"They had firebombs of some type. See, what we did in tunnels was use a flamethrower and burn out anyone inside, but they were ready and firebombed the men with the thrower, sending the flame back. It was a real mess."

"Is that what you couldn't tell me?" Morgan asked.

"The details of the entire mission are classified, as far as I know. I'm probably in violation of God knows how many laws or acts by telling you this in the first place. Angus said he was going to look into the families of the men who were killed, but he didn't find anything as far as I know. I'm sure he would have said something if he had."

"Is that it?" Morgan asked.

"Isn't that enough?"

Morgan took his hands. "Richie, you didn't do anything wrong. You were given information by someone you trusted and who should have known better. He's the one who's responsible for those men, and the Marines said the same thing."

"But you weren't there to see them hurt and burned. You didn't have to witness it, and you certainly aren't seeing them in your dreams every night."

"No, I'm not. I see the people I didn't get to in time. Hindsight is always perfect. You know that. Do the other men in your unit blame you?"

"Snoop, I talked to him yesterday, he says they don't, but…."

"Stop blaming yourself for what you didn't have control over. The other men in the unit have forgiven you for whatever happened, and maybe it's time you forgave yourself. Guilt is pretty powerful—it turns the good things bad and makes the bad things worse."

"How poetic," Richie countered.

"Can you argue with it, or do you have only smartass quips?" Morgan challenged. "Because if you think about it, you know I'm right. Bad things happen in war, just like awful things can happen in a fire. We do our best, and that's all we can do." Morgan paused, becoming completely still. "Is that all there is to it?"

"Yes," Richard said. "I don't lie." God, that hurt more than he would ever have thought.

"You've been evasive, and now you tell me everything."

"That's because I told you I'd tell you what happened, and I have." He pushed back from the table and took his plate, barely touched, over to the sink. "They classified the mission and put out their own story of what happened, making the rebels look lucky and us less incompetent. But that doesn't change what happened."

Morgan got up and walked over to the sink. "I didn't mean to question your ethics."

"Then why did you?" Richard asked, very hurt. He'd told the story he never wanted to have to tell again, and damn, it cut deep that Morgan hadn't fully believed him.

"I don't know."

That seemed like a lame answer, and Richard wasn't sure he believed Morgan. God, this was turning into as big a mess of hurt and guilt as he'd been afraid of in the first place. "I didn't want to tell you because I hate talking about it. I had to tell the story dozens of times, and with every retelling I felt more and more useless and like a bigger and bigger failure." And fuck all if he didn't feel that same way again. He'd trusted Morgan with his story, the one he kept closed and within himself, and Morgan hadn't believed him.

"You aren't a failure, and yes, what happened was tragic." Morgan turned him away from the sink and knelt in front of his chair before hugging him tightly. "This whole thing is tragic, what happened as well as how they left you feeling. Tribunals and courts-martial are all about trying to get to the facts and finding out who was responsible, but they rarely consider what they've done to the people involved. Rip people apart to get at the truth, and then once it's over everyone is supposed to go back to the way things were as though nothing had happened. They didn't find that you were at fault, so everything was fine as far as they were concerned."

"But I could have stopped it."

"Could you? If you had checked and found out something different than the intelligence you were given, would they have changed or halted the mission? Would your commander simply have dismissed it and given the order to go ahead anyway?" Morgan was so insistent. "You don't know and never will. But he was the one who assigned the mission, and he gave you the intelligence. You may have been the leader, but it sounds to me like you were given bad information and ordered into a situation that you had little choice but to accept."

"But...."

"You were set up for failure," Morgan said. "It's that simple. Others made mistakes, and you paid for them with your ability to walk and your friends' lives."

Richard lowered his head, and Morgan instantly cradled it.

"I led them all to their deaths," Richard whispered through a clenched throat as he tried to stop the outpouring of grief, fear, and even relief that welled up and burst out of him like a geyser. Morgan held him tightly as he shook and tried not to cry like a child but failed miserably. Richard had told his story, and finally, by some miracle, Morgan hadn't condemned him for it.

"It was war, and you followed the orders you were given, and I'm sure that once you realized what was happening, you did whatever you could to get your men out."

"I did, but it was too late," Richard gasped and then gulped hard as words failed him and he went to pieces in Morgan's arms. He was a Marine, damn it, and Marines didn't cry like babies. Richard tried to get himself under control, but he couldn't do anything about the flow of grief that nearly overwhelmed him for all the men who had been lost. Richard held Morgan as the acute loss for each man stabbed at him like it was yesterday.

"What am I supposed to do?" Richard gasped.

"I think you've already started," Morgan said softly into his ear and slowly wound his fingers through his hair.

It felt like it was the day after the battle when he had lain in the hospital more worried about the men than the fact that he couldn't move his legs. "Afterwards I was in the hospital, and I kept asking about the men who were with me and found out one by one what had happened to them. Each piece of news was—"

He clamped his eyes closed as the scenes played in his mind like a horror movie. Snoop was in the bed next to him, and thankfully he wasn't hurt as badly as Richard seemed to have been. "I always thought losing my legs was penance for what happened."

"It doesn't work that way. At least that's what I like to think. We don't get afflicted with disease or lose the use of limbs as retaliation for the things we think we've done." Morgan held him so close. "Just let it all out. Once you do you can deal with it… we can deal with it together."

Richard had no idea one single word could have such an impact. We. A small, tiny word that meant so much, that he wasn't alone and that he had someone he could count on to be there for him. "What do I do now?"

"First thing is to calm down, and maybe we find you someone professional to speak with."

Richard tensed and pulled away. "I've had enough of them."

"You need someone to help you deal with what happened. I can listen, but I'm not a therapist, and they have techniques and things you can do to help yourself. That's the key, putting you in control of yourself rather than the dreams."

"Maybe," Richard said as he began getting control of his emotions.

He sniffed and wished he had a tissue. Morgan handed him a napkin, and he wiped his nose, feeling a little like a wrung-out child.

"You need to eat and try not to think about all this right now," Morgan told him and led him back to the table. He got another plate and silverware, dished out some more dinner and put it in the microwave for a few seconds. He reheated his plate as well and then began to eat once again.

Richard picked at his food as his appetite returned slowly. "They tell me the dreams will probably never stop," Richard said.

"That's true. I know that, but they could become less frequent if you deal with the pain that caused them in the first place." Morgan continued eating, shoveling in the food as though he were starved. "What about your friend, Snoop, wasn't it? What did he say?"

"They didn't blame me."

"Had you talked to any of them before?"

Richard shook his head.

"Why?"

"I couldn't face them. How could I look any of them in the eye after what happened? I was in a hospital and then flown stateside. Most were still deployed, and I blamed myself…."

"And thought they did too?"

Morgan seemed so understanding, it was starting to blow Richard's mind.

"Yeah." He took another bite and did his best to chew and swallow, but he really didn't taste anything. "I really screwed this whole thing up, didn't I?"

"No. You have a good heart and took on more than you had to. Regardless of what you think, you're only responsible for what was in your control." Morgan waved his empty fork. "A few years ago there was a huge fire in Carlisle that we all got called to. It was at an old factory, and the place was massive. They'd made carpets, and the place was supposed to be empty, but it wasn't. Someone had stored chemicals in part of the building, probably old ones that never got cleared out, and they went up, taking most of that part of the building along with them. We arrived just in time to see the explosion. Bricks, glass, wall, steel, it all went everywhere."

"Was anyone hurt?"

"Yeah, a firefighter died. He was too close to that part of the structure, and one of the large pieces of masonry crushed him. The entire department there went into mourning, and I understand that the captain who sent him out there resigned because of it. He hung up his hat and pants permanently."

"But it wasn't his fault," Richard said and groaned as soon as the words left his mouth. "Son of a…."

"Yeah. Guilt sucks, and it cost the Carlisle department a seasoned veteran because he couldn't deal with it any longer. It wasn't his fault, but the fault of the people who didn't clean out the building. Still, he couldn't live with it."

"You're a sneaky bastard."

"I've been called worse." He smiled and finished his dinner. "I'm going to check outside to see what was going on." Morgan pushed back the chair. "Oh, before I forget, one of the guys at the station has some puppies that need homes. They're golden retriever pups, and I was wondering if you'd like one."

Richard turned to where Morgan stood by the back door. "Don't you mean that you want a puppy?"

"No. I'm asking if you'd like it if we got a puppy."

There was that first person plural again, and it wasn't the first time Morgan had used it.

"Morgan, you know I can't stay here forever. That isn't fair to you and…."

"Do you want to leave? I thought you liked it here."

There were so many things wrong with that question. "I do like it here. That isn't the point. You rescued me from a fire and then basically took me home because I didn't have a place to go. I can't expect to live here permanently." He wasn't sure if he was saying that for Morgan's sake or his own. It wasn't realistic, and even though his gut clenched at the thought of leaving, he had to make plans to get on with his life. He also couldn't be dependent on Morgan.

"Why the hell not? I added a ramp and will put one on the back as well. You can stay in your own room if you want and…."

"Are you asking me to live with you?"

"Am I speaking English? Of course I am. I have room, and I like having you here with me. If it will make you feel better, you can chip in for utilities and stuff." Morgan let go of the doorknob. "You're my other half."

"How can you know that?" Richard asked, a little floored.

"I knew it when we were thirteen. Why do you think I fell apart after I left? You were my best friend and the person who knew me best, and you still do."

"Are you sure?"

Morgan strode across the floor, turned the chair, placed his hands on the arms, and looked Richard straight in the eyes without moving. "You look me in the eyes and tell me what you want most in the world. Be honest and say it."

"Pretty sure of yourself."

"No," Morgan said, staring without moving. "I'm very sure of you."

Richard looked back into Morgan's deep brown eyes, afraid of what he might see and also scared to look away. The intensity hit him like a boulder rushing down a raging rapids, propelled by water with too much force to stop it. "Morgan...."

"Richie. You are my husband, remember? We were married years ago, and I know we were playing, but that stayed with me always. There hasn't been anyone else to get close because no one else was you."

"We were young."

"But the heart wants what the heart wants."

Morgan didn't look away for a second, even as he leaned closer and closer until Richard felt the heat from his lips touch his.

"I've told you before. All you have to do is decide what you want and say it."

"But how can I do that when you're this close, and I can't think?" Richard swallowed hard, Morgan's scent surrounding him, rich and heavy, settling on him the way cigarette smoke clings to clothes. Come to think of it, Richard wanted Morgan's scent to surround him and hoped that intoxicating aroma never faded.

"Thinking is overrated. Try feeling. Close your mind and open your heart. It will tell you what to do."

Morgan didn't come any closer. Richard balanced on the edge of the proverbial knife, deciding if what his heart told him was real or simply an illusion. Everything Morgan had to offer him was too good to believe. Yet it was all he wanted.

Before he could think twice or stop it, Richard leaned forward, bringing their lips together, and all else was forgotten.

Morgan enclosed him in a hug, holding him in thick arms that cradled him in comfort and heat that built by the second. He pressed harder, deepening the kiss as he parted his lips, dueling with Morgan's probing tongue. Damn, that was magic, and it inflamed him even more.

Richard squirmed in his chair, rocking slightly back and forth as their passion grew and he couldn't contain it any longer. The need for relief nearly had him sliding out of the chair and onto the floor so Morgan could take him right then and there. Richard gasped when Morgan pulled back, whimpering in his need for more.

"I need to check outside before my brain completely fries."

"But…," Richard sputtered, blinking to clear the lust-filled haze from his head. ·

"I'll be right back to pick up where we left off, but if I don't do this now, it will get too dark." Morgan hurried to the door. "If I let you distract me one more time, I'll never get this done."

He was out the door so fast that Richard wondered what the hell he'd done.

Thankfully his wonder didn't last long. Morgan bounded back in, closed the door, and locked it. Richard instantly felt Morgan's heated gaze on him.

"There's nothing out there," Morgan said, his words immaterial when he never looked away.

He could have said that the house was flooding and about to wash away. Richard wouldn't have noticed.

Morgan strode over to him and bent down. This time it wasn't for a kiss. Morgan placed one arm under Richard's knees and the other behind his back and lifted him out of the chair.

"Come on, sweetheart." Morgan hefted him up and walked down the hall.

"Are you going all caveman on me?"

"You better believe it."

Morgan pushed open the door to his bedroom and set Richard on the bed. Then, without a word, he stripped Richard of every stitch of clothing. Fuck, it was exciting and a little uncomfortable in a good way, with him naked and Morgan still dressed.

"Damn, I love that."

Morgan raked his gaze down every inch of Richard's increasingly heated body, stopping at his cock, which throbbed and bounced against his belly. Morgan's eyes promised heat and passion beyond his wildest dreams.

Chapter 7

MORGAN FEASTED his eyes on Richie. After laying him on the bed, he couldn't move an inch because Richie took his breath away. He was far from perfect, his physical scars marring his skin in a way that was uniquely Richie. No one else would ever be like him, and those scars and wounds were gotten in battle and earned through hardship and pain. That in itself was sexy.

"Damn." His eyes settled on Richie's long, thick cock straining on his belly.

"Morgan, I'm starting to feel a little self-conscious."

"Nope," Morgan countered. "I want to look my fill, and damn it, I'm going to." He leaned over the bed and captured Richie's lips, cradling his head in his hand so he could control the incredible pressure on their lips.

Richie quivered beneath him as Morgan continued the kiss and let one hand roam over his chest and down his belly. When Morgan reached Richie's cock, he encircled it and held tight, listening to Richie's throaty moans that had his own cock throbbing in his pants, which grew tighter by the second. When he straightened up, Morgan pulled his gray T-shirt over his head and then popped the button on his jeans. He wasn't in the mood to do a striptease, and Richie seemed about ready to rip his clothes off anyway, so he stripped and climbed onto the bed.

Richie rolled onto his side, and Morgan helped him until he was on top, staring into Morgan's eyes. "I'm in charge now." Richie cupped his cheeks. "You were so mean, making me wait like that." He flexed his hips, sliding his cock along Morgan's in a delicious surge of amazingness. Morgan cupped Richie's ass, pressing the two of them together, encouraging Richie to do whatever he wanted.

"You know this can be awkward sometimes. Sex isn't smooth or graceful with me."

"Sex is never as graceful or artistic as it is in the movies," Morgan said. "It's messy, sometimes clunky, and with you, always an amazing journey that I want to be able to take as many times as you'll let me. And if you ask me why, I'm going to paddle your sweet tight butt right now." He lightly tapped his hand on Richie's cheek.

"I'm not into that," he squeaked and then cut off further conversation by kissing Morgan's breath away.

During sex, Morgan had been the aggressor, the one in charge, and it really fit his personality. He also suspected that Richie needed to be in control right now, so Morgan suppressed his natural urge to take over. Fucking hell, was he glad he did. Richie was a natural, and he played him like he was hitting a home run. Richie may not have had the use of his legs, but he made up for it with his fingers, hands, lips, and tongue.

He was right, of course. Things between them were a little clunky at times, but patience had its rewards, and Richie more than made up for not being able to move easily, especially when he parted his sweet lips and took Morgan in his mouth, sucking him deep enough to take away Morgan's ability to think.

Richie swirled his tongue and sucked on the head, flicking that spot just below until Morgan clutched at the bedding with near abandon. "You're good at that."

Richie beamed and sucked him deep again. That look was nearly enough to send him over the edge. Richie happy and smiling was a sight to behold, and his cock sliding between Richie's lips was the sexiest sight on earth.

"Richie… I'm close…."

He sucked harder. Morgan managed to hold off and cupped Richie's cheeks, moving him off.

"Morgan."

"I'm not ready, sweetheart." He kissed him. "Do you think you can… top me?" He wasn't sure what Richie was comfortable with and didn't want to push.

"Me?"

"Yeah." Morgan kissed him. "I want to feel you." He helped Richie roll onto his side and then got some lube and a condom from the bedside table. He took a few seconds to prepare himself and handed Richie the condom.

Richie's hand shook as he rolled on the condom. Morgan couldn't lie down until he'd watched him roll the latex down his cock. Morgan lay on his side and helped Richie get into position.

When Richie breached him, he gasped and grunted as the stretch overwhelmed him. He needed all that Richie could give him, and as Richie filled him, he got just that. "I want to see you," Richie whispered from behind him, and Morgan clamped his muscles around Richie's cock and felt him scrape his teeth over his shoulder.

"I want that too," Morgan whispered and slowly moved away, gasping when Richie slipped from inside him. "Roll onto your back," Morgan said softly and then straddled Richie, lowering his body onto him. Now they could see each other, and Morgan got to look into Richie's eyes and see the gleam of passion and wide-pupiled happiness. "I love you, Richie," Morgan said as he lifted himself and sank back down.

Richie gasped, and Morgan didn't know the exact cause, but either way it was because of him, and that was good enough.

"Morgan…."

Richie grasped his thighs, holding on while Morgan leaned back and rode Richie like the stallion he was. It didn't matter that Richie couldn't use his legs. He was a stallion, this raging, riding, strong and thunderous stud of a man. When Richie grasped his cock, stroking and letting him thrust up and down, Morgan's heart and mind flew all the way to the clouds. This was pure physical perfection, and it was all Richie.

"Jesus," Richie groaned, moving his hips upward.

He didn't have the greatest amount of movement, but Morgan made up for what Richie lacked. Not that it mattered, because Richie had enthusiasm, and the way his mouth hung open and his eyes glazed over was so fucking sexy. That alone was almost enough to send Morgan over the edge he was approaching way too fast.

He wanted this to last for as long as possible, but his own excitement and needs betrayed him, and Morgan groaned loudly, holding on to the last semblance of his control.

"Morgan, I'm coming!"

"That's it, sweetheart. I wanna feel it!" He pounded as hard as he dared, replacing Richie's hand with his own as he stroked himself to completion seconds after he felt Richie coming inside him.

Morgan didn't float after sex, not this time. He'd taken off like a rocket, and now he hung in midair, on the edge of a breath until he crashed back into himself with a gasp. He didn't want to hurt Richie, but his energy was totally shot.

Morgan ended up lying next to Richie on the bed, sucking in air, unable to talk. Time stood still. He had no idea how long he lay there and didn't care. Richie eventually reached over to him, their hands locking together, fingers interlacing, neither wanting this to be over.

"Let me get a cloth," Morgan said, unmoving still.

"Yeah," Richie breathed. "Too bad we can't just have one come to us."

"Maybe if we get a dog, we can train him," Morgan said.

"Ewww, I'm sorry, but if we get a dog, he is staying outside during sex and all amorous activity. I don't do shows, especially not for four-legged audiences."

Richie smacked him lightly on the chest, and Morgan knew it was probably time to get up. He groaned as he did so and went to the bathroom, where he wetted a cloth with warm water and returned, cleaning up Richie and taking care of the condom.

"I really like having you in my bed," Morgan said as he climbed under the light covers. "You look really good there."

Richie hesitated to answer. "Sometimes I don't know if you're serious or teasing."

"I'd never tease about something like that." Morgan rolled onto his side, lightly stroking Richie's belly, lightly tracing the occasional old scar. In places there were so many of them. Most were small, but they were there nonetheless.

"Why do you do that?" Richie asked as he shimmied away.

"Does touching them hurt?" Morgan asked as he pulled his hand back.

"No, but…."

Morgan held Richie's gaze and went back to what he was doing, feeling Richie relax. Morgan knew Richie needed to understand that as far as he was concerned, there was nothing about Richie that wasn't attractive. He'd tried explaining, but now he thought he needed to let his hands do the talking. Words only went so far, but touch made an even deeper impression. Morgan pushed the covers away and sat up, leaning over Richie. A scar ran along his left hip, and he kissed along the length.

"That tickles," Richie said through stifled laughter.

Morgan increased the pressure and continued kissing down the length of the scar. Then he transferred to one on Richie's shoulder, followed by his legs. "Your scars are part of you and the man you are. They're not something to be hidden or ashamed of, least of all with me." He lifted his gaze to Richie's. "Do you understand?"

Richie nodded slowly, biting his lower lip. Morgan knew that scars could feel different from other skin and expected what he was doing might feel weird to Richie.

"Can you tell me how it feels when I touch your legs?" He ran his hand from thigh to ankle.

"When it first happened, I had very little feeling. Now it's like there's a fog around them, and I'm feeling your hands through that. You could grip them tightly, and it might feel like a normal touch. It's hard to gauge anymore because my sense memory is fading as well. If you will, my legs are forgetting what it was like to be touched before the accident."

"But if you can feel, why can't you walk?"

"They said it's because I only have part of my spinal cord at the base. I'm pretty lucky that things work during sex. They didn't for a while, but they do now. For six months I had to wear catheters and things like that. They were hopeful when I started progressing that I might regain more of my usage, but then it stopped and wouldn't go any further no matter what I did." Richie groaned softly. "That feels kind of good."

"I'm pressing rather hard and don't want to be any firmer, but I'm glad."

"One doctor said that the reason I wasn't progressing was in my mind, and another of the doctors was so angry with him, he pulled him from my case. I heard later that that was his answer for every case he couldn't help. Bastard."

"So you'll never walk again?" Morgan asked.

"Some doctors say there's a chance while others say it's unlikely at this point. I try to move my feet and legs all the time but don't have any luck. I used to think if I could move my toes I could walk and have one of those 'movie of the week' kind of stories, but I don't think that's possible."

"Do you want to try? We can go to one of those therapy places and find a doctor to examine you. We'd have to be careful."

"Is that what you want me to do?" Richie asked.

Morgan shrugged. "Doesn't matter what I want. It's all about what you want to do. You know your body better than I do. Though I'm hoping that soon I'll be able to give you a run for your money." Morgan flashed what he hoped was a wicked smile, then crawled back up under the covers.

But his nonstop day quickly caught up with him, and as much as he'd have liked to be able to spend time talking to Richie, his eyelids drooped, and he soon fell asleep.

MORGAN ENDED up working extra shifts. The station was shorthanded because of a strain of flu that seemed to be making the rounds. The good news was that Henry had been released from the hospital and was home with his family. It would be a while before he could return to work, but at least his injuries weren't as bad as initially thought.

"We appreciate you coming in," Captain Rogers said as he made a pass through the station on his way to the office. "I believe someone will come in at noon and we can send you home."

The overtime was nice, but he'd been hoping to spend some time with Richie. And apparently when he went home, he'd have a little bundle of energy to take home with him. The guys were currently playing with the eight-week-old golden retriever pup, and Morgan was starting to wonder if he was going to get out of the station with the little guy.

"Hey, Angus, what brings you by?" Morgan asked as he descended the stairs to get to work and check on the puppy he planned to bring home to Richie. "There hasn't been another fire, has there?"

"No. That's what's worrying me. It's been too long. These guys don't usually just go quiet. They have an agenda and a need that only the flames will satisfy."

"How can I help you?" He motioned to one of the small equipment rooms where they could talk privately.

"I don't know. There was something fishy with the last fire, and I can't put my finger on it. Something is different, but…." He walked to the small window and peered out. "With the first fire, we think there was gasoline on the exterior, but the fire went inside too fast, so something had to have been gotten in the house."

"Like a Molotov cocktail?" Morgan asked.

"Yeah. We didn't find any evidence of that at the failed attempt on your house, but they may not have gotten to that point. I'm still trying to reason that one out. The thing is, there was nothing at the last fire."

Morgan leaned against one of the equipment tables. "Okay." He wasn't sure where Angus was going with this line of reasoning.

"It was like he set the place on fire but didn't really care. He wasn't as invested in the outcome." Angus motioned with his hands as he spoke. "I've spent days trying to find a connection between the last victim and either Richie or Grace and her family, and there is none. Nothing, zip."

"So…." An idea formed in Morgan's head that made his skin crawl. "What are you saying?"

"That either the last fire wasn't done by the same person like we thought or it could have been a diversion, some sort of red herring to throw us off the track. I was looking at this case as though the arsonist was single-minded and intent on only one thing. Maybe he is, but the guy is also devious and willing to burn out someone's home in order to throw us off the trail."

"You really think that's what happened?" Morgan asked, his hands tingling as the blood rushed away from them.

"Call part of it gut feeling and intuition. The truth is, I don't have much of any proof. The guy could have figured he didn't need the Molotovs, or it could be something else…."

"Someone was at the house yesterday, and Mitzy scared them off. Kevin was there with Richie. I didn't see anything and thought they were overreacting a little." His leg started shaking. "If you're right and that fire was a red herring, then it's likely that whoever's behind this is after Richie after all." His chest went tight, and he grabbed his phone.

The number rang without being answered. Morgan left a message and then called right back. This time the call went straight to voice mail like it had been shut off. "He's not answering." Morgan called the house number, and it just rang and rang. "Something's wrong. Richie always keeps his phone with him."

Angus had already pulled open the door to the storage room. "What are we waiting for?" Angus tilted his head toward the exit, and Morgan was out like a shot. He checked in with Captain Rogers just long enough to give him the briefest rundown on what they thought was going on.

"You call us and the police if you find anything."

He wanted to catch this guy as badly as the rest of the department did. Morgan thanked him and was out the door and in his car with Angus in the passenger seat in a matter of seconds.

"Slow down a little. You're going to run someone over," Angus said, holding on to the strap by the door as Morgan drove as fast as he dared.

He pulled to a stop in front of the neighbor's house across the street. The house looked normal. There was no smoke rising, and the open windows in the bedroom weren't belching the smoke he half expected to see. Richie's car was parked where it had been when he left. Everything seemed normal, and yet he knew something was different. His skin crawled, and Morgan gripped the steering wheel so tightly his knuckles turned white. "Do you think he's in there?" Morgan asked, looking up and down the street. There were cars parked randomly on the street, some he recognized and a few he didn't.

"We can call the police," Angus offered as Morgan opened his door and got out of the car.

"Go through the neighbor's yard and see if anyone is in back of the house. They work during the day, so no one is home."

"What are you going to do?"

"Take the other way. We'll meet behind the house." Morgan used the sidewalk, trying not to seem like he was attempting to look in the front window. He didn't see anything and continued to the neighbor's before doubling back around and making it to the open back door.

"You were the one responsible," he heard a strange voice say. Morgan pressed flat to the house. He wasn't sure what to do at that moment.

"I was in charge, but it was old intelligence, and I didn't know how bad it was going to be." Richie's voice was steady and strong, cool under pressure.

"My brother, the only family I had left, died because of you. He burned to death. When they got him home, there was nothing but black in that coffin. You burned up the only person who meant

anything to me. He was all I had, and now… poof… he's gone."
Anger and pain came through the screen door like a black cloud.

"You set the fires," Richie said.

"Oh yeah. That first house I thought I got closer to you, but I
messed up, and you got out. I watched, and when I didn't see you,
I thought I'd gotten you and that you'd burned up like my brother.
But no…. You were saved by that do-gooder firefighter."

Morgan heard flesh meet flesh in a sharp smack, and he had to
stop himself from rushing in there. He didn't know if the guy had
a gun or not.

Slowly Morgan inched away from the door and continued
around the house. He peered around the corner and saw Angus. He
made dialing motions with his hands, and Angus nodded and began
backing away. Morgan inched back near the door.

The level of tension coming through the screen door was
palpable.

"It was all you, and don't try to tell me otherwise. I tried to
get to you at that hospital, but they had people watching all the
time, and it was then that I knew I'd follow you and do to you what
you did to my brother."

Morgan chanced a look inside, but he couldn't really see
what was happening. They must have been just out of visual range
from the door. That also meant they couldn't see him, at least for
the moment. He was well aware that one sound and he'd give
himself away. Morgan backed away once again and hoped that
help got here before this guy decided to start pouring gasoline or
something.

Morgan could have kicked himself. He'd been so focused
on Richie and what was happening inside that he hadn't really
looked around. A gas can sat right near the neighboring house. One
that wasn't his. He wasn't sure if it was the Wilsons' either, but
he quietly went over and lifted the full can. Morgan swore under
his breath and carefully went back the way he came, taking the
gasoline with him. If this belonged to the arsonist, he somehow

doubted that it was all he'd brought, but at least he hoped he'd lessened his arsenal.

"I called the police and the department," Angus said when he met him. "I'll take care of this."

He took the can, and Morgan crept back to the screen door.

"…not taking any chances this time."

Morgan's gut and fists clenched. He wondered if he should bust in and see if he could take care of this guy.

"I'm not lighting the outside of the house."

A metal *ting* left Morgan cold.

"I'm going to use you as the fire starter, then flick a match and go. I get to watch you burn just like my brother did, and then I'll be long gone."

The guy tapped the dull metal again, and the image of an old metal gas can flashed in Morgan's mind. The sound was dull and lifeless because the damn can was full.

Morgan wished help would get here. He was scared to death that this guy was going to start pouring gasoline at any second.

"What was your brother's name?" Richie asked.

"Gregory," the guy answered.

"Hardmore?" Richie asked. "My God. He was such a good man. I remember him so well, and I mourned him when I heard he was gone."

"You fucking did not!"

"I did. I knew every man who died, and I wished to hell they hadn't."

Damn. Morgan wasn't sure if what Richie was saying was true, but it nearly had him in tears.

"That same mission left me like this, and I've felt it's my punishment for what happened. I'll never walk again no matter what happens."

"You… you… you were in charge. It was you who was responsible."

The man's voice wavered. If they got out of this, Richie had a future as a hostage negotiator if he wanted it.

"I was only following my orders, the same as your brother was. We all were."

Morgan knew the hell Richie had gone through just to begin to understand and process what had happened.

"Just go. Take your can and get out of the house. Go where you want and live your life. No one has been hurt so far."

That was brilliant, giving the guy a way out. Morgan began moving away from the door in case he took Richie up on his offer. He figured he could grab the guy as soon as he stepped outside the house and Richie was safe.

Sirens sounded, and they got closer fast. Morgan clamped his eyes closed, wishing they'd been a few minutes later.

"You called the police!" the guy yelled from inside. "You lied to me!" It was all coming apart. Panic rang in his voice as the sirens got even closer, stopping just outside the house.

Skin hit skin again, and then Morgan heard the unmistakable sound of a scuffle followed by someone hitting the floor. All Morgan could see in his mind was that the guy had pulled Richie out of his chair and had him on the floor, pouring gasoline while he stood here, waiting. Screw it. Morgan yanked the back door open and raced inside.

Richie was on the ground, but so was the other guy, with Richie holding him down.

"Don't go hitting me, you stupid son of a bitch. I'm a Marine like your brother was, and just because I'm in some stupid chair doesn't mean I'm not lethal." He held the man's arms behind his back.

"Damn it, you're hurting me."

"You're lucky I don't break your fucking arms."

"Angus," Morgan called at the top of his lungs, and he raced inside and skidded to a halt at the scene in front of him. "Get the police in here, and tell them we have the arsonist in custody." Morgan grinned. Damn, Richie was something else.

The police rushed inside, and they all stopped in their tracks for a second, seemingly a little confused.

"This is the arsonist," Richie said.

"Are you sure?" one of the officers asked.

"Antonio," Angus began, "this is Richie. He's a Marine, and this is the guy who's been setting our fires."

"I heard his whole confession," Morgan said. "It's probably best that you get him out of here, along with the can of gasoline." The scent was strong, and Morgan wondered if he'd poured some on the house. Morgan didn't see where the floor was wet, but the spout on the can was open, so that may have been the source of the smell.

An officer snapped pictures and then removed the gasoline can while another got the arsonist to his feet. Morgan knelt down and helped Richie up before cradling him in his arms and lifting him into the chair.

"You're all right."

"How much did you hear?" Richie asked.

"Probably the last five minutes or so. No more. He had more gasoline outside that we got away." He reluctantly looked away from Richie. "His car has to be nearby, and he will probably have more in it."

"He's made up Molotov cocktails before," Angus said to Antonio, who ordered men to search the guy and then find his car.

"Did he hurt you?" Morgan asked Richie, who shook his head.

"Not really." Richie settled in the chair. "How did you know he was here?"

"Angus and his intuition. He figured out that the last fire was different and may have been a decoy. Then it all came back to you. Mitzy probably scared him away yesterday, and when I called and you didn't answer, I got worried."

"He took my phone after the first call."

"That was his mistake. I got worried, and Angus and I raced over." He was so relieved that Richie was safe he could hardly believe it. "When I heard someone fall to the floor, I thought it was you."

"He tried to pull me out of the chair, but I used my weight to take him with me. He wasn't ready for that, and I was able to take him by surprise. That was pretty awesome."

"Did you really know his brother?" Morgan asked.

"I did. The guy was a nutcase just like his brother. He didn't deserve what happened to him, though. None of them did."

Richie grew quiet, and Morgan could feel him pulling away.

"We need to talk to both of you," Antonio told them and motioned for Morgan to come with him while another officer sat next to Richie.

"You heard this guy?" Antonio asked.

"Yeah, he set all three fires and attempted the one on the house here. He wanted revenge for his brother's death. You'll have to ask Richie for any information he can give you."

"How did you know to come home?" Antonio asked, making notes. "And I've already talked a minute to Angus and am well aware of his intuitions."

"Then let's say I got the same feeling when Richie didn't answer his phone, so we raced over here."

"He's never going to let me live down giving him shit the other week over his last hunch. That one turned out to be nothing." He made a few more notes. "Is there anything else you want to tell me?"

"Angus can tell you where he put the other gas can, though I will say that I wasn't careful when I touched it. I just wanted to get it away from the house."

"Great. That evidence will likely be useless, but be sure to leave your fingerprints so we can rule them out." He seemed really pissed off about something.

"We got the guy, Detective," Morgan said. "Isn't that what counts?"

"Yeah. Except I'm going to get more shit about firefighters catching the bad guys before I can even get there." He turned to leave the room, lowering his notebook into his pocket.

"We're all on the same side," Morgan told him, but Antonio continued walking away.

"Sometimes he can be a real jackass," Angus said quietly from behind him. "The two of us went out for a while, but it wasn't going to work out. He's a good detective, just gets a little too wrapped up in his own ego sometimes."

"If you say so," Morgan said and went in search of Richie. He came out of the bathroom a minute later.

"Are they done with you?" Morgan asked.

"For now, I guess. I suspect I'm going to have to testify, and I'm going to need to call the Marines to find out what I can say on the stand about my mission. Court records will make it public. They'll probably assign me a lawyer to help sort out that part of the mess."

"Are you all okay?" Captain Rogers asked as the house filled with firefighters.

"Yes. Can you have someone check that no gasoline was actually spilled in the house? That's the last thing we need."

"Certainly."

The captain looked at one of the men, who raced outside, most likely to get a test kit. When he returned, the guys checked various areas of the carpet and kitchen.

"It's clean, Captain," Riggs said.

"Thanks, man."

"No problem. Can't have gas fumes building up in the house." Riggs clapped him on the shoulder and took the kit away. "I'd say you've had enough excitement for the day," Riggs told Morgan. "We're going to take off, and we'll see you in a few days for your shift. Mr. Smalley, you did a great job taking care of this guy." He smiled at Richie, and then they all trooped out of the house.

One by one, the fire trucks and squad cars pulled away. Angus got a ride back with them, leaving the two of them alone.

"Are you sure you're okay?" Morgan asked. He really wanted to strip Richie down and see for himself.

"I'm fine."

"Did you hurt your legs when you tumbled to the floor?"

"No. Falling is something I do pretty well now. It's getting up that's the real problem." Richie was trying to make jokes.

"Real funny." Morgan wasn't in the mood. "I will say, you taking on this guy was the last thing I suspected." He leaned close, lightly tugging on Richie's ear with his lips. "It was really hot."

"So wrestling does it for you? I always knew you had a kink somewhere."

"I think my kink, if I have one, is you." Morgan let go of the last of his nerves and kissed Richie gently. "Crap," he muttered when he broke away.

"Was it that bad?'

"No," Morgan said, chuckling. "I had a surprise for you at the station, and I left it there in all the excitement." He was going to need to go back and get him for Richie.

"Guys," Angus called through the front door as Morgan was getting ready to leave. He'd checked the property once more for good measure and wondered how long it would be before he'd be able to go anywhere without walking the foundations of the house to look for possible incendiary devices. "I think you left something."

Morgan opened the door, and Angus pushed the squirming puppy into his arms.

"I brought the rest of his things. I'll get them from the car."

"Thanks, I really appreciate it." Morgan held the puppy close as he wriggled and tried to lick his face. When he turned around, he handed him to Richie. "I thought he'd help keep you company when I'm gone, and when he gets older he'll help keep both of us safe."

"What's his name?" Richie asked as he tried to keep his face out of the range of puppy tongue.

"He doesn't have one yet. I thought you could name him."

Morgan smiled as Richie set the pup on his lap, and he settled enough to be petted for a few seconds. Then he stood, tail wagging, looking at Morgan with fascinated interest.

"I need to get back, but you two have fun."

Angus set the bag of puppy things near the door and left. Morgan doubted Richie even heard him—his attention was fixated on the bundle of energy and adoration in his lap.

"What should we call you?" Richie asked, and the pup turned around, slathering Richie's face when he got too close. "Any ideas?"

"Mr. Wiggle Bottom comes to mind," Morgan fake groused. "Or Mr. Licky Face."

"Those are terrible names, aren't they?" Richie asked the puppy, who tried to lick him again.

Maybe Morgan was going to need to be jealous of the puppy's attention-getting ability.

"How about Lucky?"

"I don't really think so," Morgan said in a fake puppy voice. "I'm more special than that."

Richie laughed and lifted the puppy into his arms, holding him under his chin. "How about Howard?" He turned the puppy to face him. "Nope, you don't look like a Howard."

Richie was clearly having fun with this, and Morgan wondered where his mind was going.

"I know… Grantham. We could call you Grant."

Richie grinned, and Morgan's mind instantly wandered.

"Why that name?" Morgan asked.

"Don't you remember?" Richie asked.

"Yeah, but I didn't think you did for some reason."

"That day in the barn after Amy's wedding, we got to ride the pony. His name was Grantham, and he loved carrots."

"Yup. Amy had her own, and we had to share, but that was fine because every time Amy got close, Grantham tried to bite her. She'd squeal and hurry away on her pony."

"Yup," Morgan agreed. "If I remember right, I swear Grantham smiled every time. That is, if a horse can smile."

"I remember that too, and watching you while you rode. You were having so much fun."

"I did. It seemed like it was the last fun I had before my dad moved us away." He leaned down. "Grant, come here."

The puppy ran over, skidding to a stop and nearly tumbling into Morgan's arms.

"I guess Grant it is." He lifted the puppy and got his face washed. He really seemed to be happy with both of them.

"I can't believe you got a puppy. I wasn't sure how serious you were."

"Of course I did. Who could take one look into this face and not get a little melty? Right, Grant?"

Morgan handed the puppy back to Richie and grabbed the bag. He set out the food and water bowls. When Richie put him down, Grant raced over to see what was in them and then set about exploring the house, sniffing everywhere. Morgan put down some papers in the kitchen and hoped he could teach the puppy to go outside pretty soon. It was going to take some time. That he knew.

"Morgan, I think we need to set some boundaries for Grant."

"Why?" Morgan asked as he stood up from putting a little food in Grant's bowl.

"Because he just came out of your room with a pair of your underwear in his mouth."

Richie was laughing, and it only continued while Morgan chased Grant around the room to get them back. Morgan got them and gave Grant a chew toy, which he seemed less interested in.

"He's going to be a handful," Morgan said without heat.

"Somehow I think he's going to take after you." Richie wheeled over to him. "You were always full of energy, and if I remember right, you were the one who led both of us into trouble."

"Me? I wasn't the one who decided it would be interesting to get in the field with the cows. Those dang things were mean." Morgan had never gotten over a fence so fast in his life.

"Okay, so maybe we were both pretty good in that department. I seem to remember a time when we snuck away with a beer you stole from your dad."

Morgan remembered that clearly. "The stuff tasted awful, and after a sip neither one of us could figure out what to do with the thing without leaving a trail. We ended up burying the whole thing and swearing each other to secrecy." God, he remembered those times so very well. He'd carried those memories through the bad years when there was very little joy in his life. He'd had friends after Richie, but none who had touched his heart or stayed with him like the times he'd had with Richie. "I sometimes wonder if you were right and I was projecting some old feelings onto you."

"No," Richie said firmly. "I think you were the one who was seeing clearly all along." He took Morgan's hand and tugged him downward. "We were friends a long time ago, but you were the friend who never left me, even when you moved away. I measured all other friendships and relationships next to that one, and they came up short."

"I know. We'd shared our deepest secrets and held them for each other."

Richie nodded. "To think kids come out of the closet at thirteen and fourteen today, and we did that back then, but only to each other."

"That's because it was right. The question is if it's still right."

"It is for me," Richie said softly, and Morgan leaned closer, meeting Richie's lips in a kiss that grew heated until paws scraped at his legs, and then Grant jumped into Richie's lap, whimpering softly. Morgan pulled away and received a lick on his face. "He doesn't want to be left out."

"There are things he's going to need to get used to."

Morgan lifted Grant and set him back on the floor. Then he returned for another kiss. Of course this time they were interrupted by a series of puppy barks and him jumping on the back of the sofa to look out the window.

"Maybe we're the ones who are going to need to get used to things being different."

"That's true. But after the last few weeks, I think I'm really starting to like things that are different."

Morgan reluctantly backed away and lifted Grant off the sofa. He scooted toward the kitchen and found what was in his bowl with enough excitement that the bowl went skittering, and some of the food spilled out onto the floor.

"Do you really think it's a good idea for us to start living together?" Richie asked.

"It's all about what you want," Morgan answered confidently. The doubt he'd always seen in Richie's eyes didn't seem to be there. It had been replaced by determination and a strength that seemed to be new, or at least had been absent for a while and was now resurging. It was amazing to see.

"I know what I want, but what do you want?" Richie asked.

"Haven't I shown you?" Morgan asked.

"Maybe you have, but it's always nice to hear the words.

"Okay," Morgan agreed with a grin. "Richie Smalley, I've wanted to spend the rest of my life with you in it since I was thirteen years old and Amy married us in the loft of her barn. I kept the ring you gave me not because I actually thought that would happen, but because I could never really let it go. So yes, I want you to be with me, in my house and in my bed. I know what it means to be a part of your life and to have you in my life." Morgan stared bullets into Richie's eyes. "So now what's your answer?"

Richie's hard expression broke into a grin. "I don't think I can compete with anything like that."

"Why don't you try," Morgan said. It felt great to tease Richie just a little.

Richie opened his mouth and then closed his lips once again. Morgan thought he might have actually stumped him until Richie grabbed his shoulders and pulled him close, then kissed him possessively. Richie sent a fizz of passion racing down his spine and heat spreading through him from head to toe.

"Is that a good enough answer?"

"I'm not sure," Morgan whispered. "Maybe I need to hear it again."

And Richie obliged over and over again until they were interrupted.

"You know, little one, you're interrupting something very important between your daddies."

"Go get a box and a blanket, and we'll put him in it. After all this running around, he'll conk out soon, and when he does, we can close the kitchen door and let him sleep while we get a nap of our own."

Morgan handed Richie the puppy and went in search of what Richie asked for. It didn't take long for him to find the box and a few towels, along with a small old blanket for warmth. He set them up in the kitchen and placed Grant inside. He turned around a few times, looking like he was figuring out what this was, and then jumped out to race around the house again.

He and Richie spent the next hour playing with the pup. At one point Morgan made a mad dash outside, catching the fountain just in time. Grant did his business and then raced across the yard chasing bugs. He let Grant play and made sure he stayed in the yard until he lay down in the grass. At that point, Morgan took him back inside and placed him in his bed. The little guy settled right down and closed his eyes.

"It's like having a baby in the house," he said quietly and pushed Richie's chair down the hall to his bedroom. "I feel like we have to be quiet or we'll wake the puppy."

"You're so cute," Richie teased, and Morgan lifted him out of the chair and set him on the edge of the bed.

He parted Richie's legs and stood between them.

"Grant is going to be fine. I, on the other hand, am feeling a little lonely."

"You are?" Morgan asked, moving right in front of Richie to get even closer. "We can't have that." He leaned down and pressed Richie back onto the mattress.

"Much better," Richie whispered as he wrapped his arms around Morgan's neck.

"Being with you is always better." He didn't want to put too much weight on Richie, but he also wanted him as close as possible. Morgan ended up slowly rolling them on the bed until Richie was on top, looking intently down at him.

"I love you," Richie said. "I really do, but I'm afraid you're getting the short end of the stick. There are many things I can't do well, and a lot of those things are going to fall to you."

"We're a team. Some things I do, some things you do, and the rest we'll figure out." Morgan lifted his head. "I do love you, Richie, and I have for almost as long as I can remember."

He leaned up for a kiss and captured Richie's lips as a yip sounded from down the hall, followed by more that got closer until a yellow streak darted into his closet, just at the edge of Morgan's sight. He groaned and reached the pup before he could get a good hold on one of Morgan's shoes. He returned to the bed, lying next to Richie and putting the puppy between them. Grant immediately settled down and curled into a ball.

"I think he only wanted to be near you," Morgan said.

"I think it was you he wanted." Richie stroked the hair off Morgan's forehead. "I know it's you that I want." Richie lifted his head, and Morgan met him over top of the pup. "I love you. I don't know exactly when it happened, but being without you is more than I think I can bear. You're part of my heart. There are many things I'm not sure of, but that isn't one of them." Richie closed the gap between them.

The future would take care of itself—for now heat and happiness reigned supreme.

Epilogue

"CAN YOU believe it's been a year?" Morgan asked as he helped Richie out of the car. "This is perfect. How did you find it?" The weathered wood holding remnants of paint nearly matched the pictures in his memories.

"Kevin helped me. He, Tristan, and Angus are all closet party planners."

Richie slid into his sleek new chair, which was featherlight and as streamlined as a spaceship. Once he was settled, Morgan opened the back door, and a very well-groomed and surprisingly behaved Grant jumped out and stood next to Richie.

Grant liked Morgan, but it was Richie he adored above everyone else. Grant listened to Richie most of all and was great company for him when Morgan was at work. Even after the threat to Richie was gone, it took Morgan a while before he didn't worry every time he left the house.

"Come on, Grant. Let's go take a look."

Richie took off with Grant, whose tail was wagging. Every now and then Grant turned to see that he was following.

"There you are," Kevin said as he came out of the barn and hurried to where Richie had stopped. "I really wanted you to see this place. I know you said you wanted to do it in a hayloft, but most barns don't have elevators."

Kevin opened the main doors, and Richie rolled inside, looking all around. Morgan stepped inside and instantly knew this was perfect.

"The barn belongs to a riding school, and right now they said they're using it for future expansion." Kevin held his arms out and twirled in a circle. "We can put the chairs right here, and they have said they will clean the stalls and have fresh hay in a few of them so it will have a fresh scent." Kevin was so excited you'd think it was his wedding they were planning.

"What do you think?" Morgan asked Richie with a smile. "It's going to be September, so it could be warm during the day. The loft would be too hot."

"I know." Richie took Morgan's hand. "I think this is perfect. It will be a small gathering anyway, and I was thinking that there were some recipes of your mother's that would go wonderfully here. Friends, some simple, good food, and you, that's all I really need."

"I'll tell them you'd like to use it."

"Have they done a wedding before?" Richie asked.

"Nope. But the couple who own the riding school are thrilled to have a wedding here. They say it will help make the place even more special." Kevin was grinning like crazy.

"How much do they want to use it for the day?"

Angus stilled Morgan's hand as he went to his pocket for a checkbook. "This is Kevin's and my gift to the two of you. It'll be all set, so just enjoy it."

"There's one more thing both of you have to see," Kevin said.

He motioned them out of the barn and up a level path through a line of trees and into a large open area in front of another barn and farmhouse, where a man and a woman came out to meet them.

"I'm Charlie, and this is Francie."

"They love the barn," Kevin said gleefully.

"Excellent. Then we'll put you on the calendar."

"That would be very nice. Thank you." Morgan could hardly believe this was happening. When he'd proposed to Richie three months ago, they'd agreed that they wanted to get married in a barn, just like the first time.

"Excellent."

Richie tugged on his hand and pointed to a corral. "Look, ponies."

Morgan nodded. "I remember."

"Did you ride?" Francie asked.

"Only as a kid." Richie took Morgan's hand. "See, Morgan and I have been married since we were thirteen years old. Our friend Amy did it, rather against our wills, you might say. It was in her barn, and we were playing." Richie tightened his grip. "Afterwards we got to ride one of the ponies that Amy's family had." He looked up at him. "I honestly think that was the last time I was on a horse."

"Me too."

"Then it's time we changed that. Part of what we do is therapy riding. So if you want to come down to the barn, we can get you set up, and you can ride."

There were tears in Richie's eyes. "Are you kidding?" There weren't many things that Richie couldn't do when he was determined.

"No. In fact, on the day of your wedding, you can ride to the ceremony if you'd like. That is, if you're comfortable."

Kevin held Grant's leash, and Francie led the way into the barn and to a special ramp that allowed Richie to get up to the level of the horse.

Francie brought around a specially saddled horse that stood stock-still. "Mable here has done this many times," Francie said, and Charlie helped Richie transfer from his chair to the back of the horse. "The saddle is designed to give you extra support."

Once he was seated and seemed steady, Richie was grinning.

"Are you ready?" Francie asked and clicked her tongue.

Mable moved forward, and Francie led the way out into a ring. Morgan followed and leaned on the rails, watching Richie ride.

"He's quite a guy," one of the barn owners said.

"Yeah, he is." Morgan turned to him. "He went to therapy for six months to try to walk again."

"Did he make progress?"

"Very little. But he stuck it out. I know he was hopeful at the beginning, but in the end he made the decision to stop and to make the most of his life. I think he's one of the bravest and strongest people I've ever met." He watched as Mable made slow revolutions of the ring with Richie. "You look good on a horse," Morgan said as Richie passed close by.

Richie sat taller and continued his ride. It was only twenty minutes or so.

"We don't want to overdo it the first time," Francie said as she led the way back inside.

They got Richie off the horse and back into his chair.

"You know, with all those months of therapy, I was really hoping I'd be able to walk down the aisle."

"Then we will," Morgan said, looking at Francie, who nodded. "We'll let the horse do the walking for you." Morgan leaned over Richie's chair, his lips right next to his. "You can have anything you want. I already got what I always wanted." Morgan leaned closer and kissed Richie a little harder than he intended and had to remember that they had an audience. "You were mine since we were kids, and you gave me this." Morgan reached into his pocket and pulled out the old ring. He took Richie's hand and slid it partway down his pinkie.

"I'm glad you knew what you wanted and didn't give up." Richie slid his hand around Morgan's neck. "I'll love you forever for that."

Richie tugged him closer, and they shared another kiss.

Morgan had often wondered if it was possible to meet your soul mate at thirteen, and now he had his answer: yes.

ANDREW GREY grew up in western Michigan with a father who loved to tell stories and a mother who loved to read them. Since then he has lived all over the country and traveled throughout the world. He has a master's degree from the University of Wisconsin-Milwaukee and now works full-time on his writing. Andrew's hobbies include collecting antiques, gardening, and leaving his dirty dishes anywhere but in the sink (particularly when writing). He considers himself blessed with an accepting family, fantastic friends, and the world's most supportive and loving husband. Andrew currently lives in beautiful historic Carlisle, Pennsylvania.

E-mail: andrewgrey@comcast.net
Website: www.andrewgreybooks.com

EYES
ONLY
FOR ME

ANDREW GREY

For years, Clayton Potter's been friends and workout partners with Ronnie. Though Clay is attracted, he's never come on to Ronnie because, let's face it, Ronnie only dates women.

When Clay's father suffers a heart attack, Ronnie, having recently lost his dad, springs into action, driving Clay to the hospital over a hundred miles away. To stay close to Clay's father, the men share a hotel room near the hospital, but after an emotional day, one thing leads to another, and straight-as-an-arrow Ronnie make a proposal that knocks Clay's socks off! Just a little something to take the edge off.

Clay responds in a way he's never considered. After an amazing night together, Clay expects Ronnie to ignore what happened between them and go back to his old life. Ronnie surprises him and seems interested in additional exploration. Though they're friends, Clay suddenly finds it hard to accept the new Ronnie and suspects that Ronnie will return to his old ways. Maybe they both have a thing or two to learn.

www.dreamspinnerpress.com

FIRE AND Snow

ANDREW GREY

Carlisle Cops: Book Four

Fisher Moreland has been cast out of his family because they can no longer deal with his issues. Fisher is bipolar and living day to day, trying to manage his condition, but he hasn't always had much control over his life and has self-medicated with whatever he could find.

JD Burnside has been cut off from his family because of a scandal back home. He moved to Carlisle but brought his Southern charm and warmth along with him. When he sees Fisher on a park bench on a winter's night, he invites Fisher to join him and his friends for a late-night meal.

At first Fisher doesn't know what to make of JD, but he slowly comes out of his shell. And when Fisher's job is threatened because of a fire, JD's support and care is more than Fisher ever thought he could expect. But when people from Fisher's past turn up in town at the center of a resurgent drug epidemic, Fisher knows they could very well sabotage his budding relationship with JD.

www.dreamspinnerpress.com

DREAMSPUN DESIRES

Andrew Grey

THE LONE RANCHER

He'll do anything to save the ranch, including baring it all.

He'll do anything to save the ranch, including baring it all.

Aubrey Klein is in real trouble—he needs some fast money to save the family ranch. His solution? A weekend job as a stripper at a club in Dallas. For two shows each Saturday, he is the star as The Lone Rancher.

It leads to at least one unexpected revelation: after a show, Garrett Lamston, an old friend from school, approaches the still-masked Aubrey to see about some extra fun… and Aubrey had no idea Garrett was gay. As the two men dodge their mothers' attempts to set them up with girls, their friendship deepens, and one thing leads to another.

Aubrey know his life stretching between the ranch and the club is a house of cards. He just hopes he can keep it standing long enough to save the ranch and launch the life—and the love—he really hopes he can have.

www.dreamspinnerpress.com

ANDREW GREY

LOVE COMES TO *Light*

A Senses Series Story

Artist Arik Bosler is terrified he might have lost his creative gift in the accident that left his hand badly burned. When he's offered the chance to work with renowned artist Ken Brighton, Arik fears his injury will be too much to overcome.

He travels to Pleasanton to meet Ken, where he runs into the intimidating Reg Thompson. Reg, a biker who customizes motorcycles, is a big man with a heart of gold who was rejected by most of his family. Arik is initially afraid of Reg because of his size. However it's Reg's heart that warms Arik's interest and gets him to look past the exterior to let down his guard.

But Arik soon realizes that certain members of Reg's motorcycle club are into things he can't have any part of. Reg can't understand why Arik disappears until he learns Arik's injury was the result of his father's drug activity. Though neither Reg nor Arik wants anything to do with drugs, the new leadership of Reg's club might have other ideas.

www.dreamspinnerpress.com

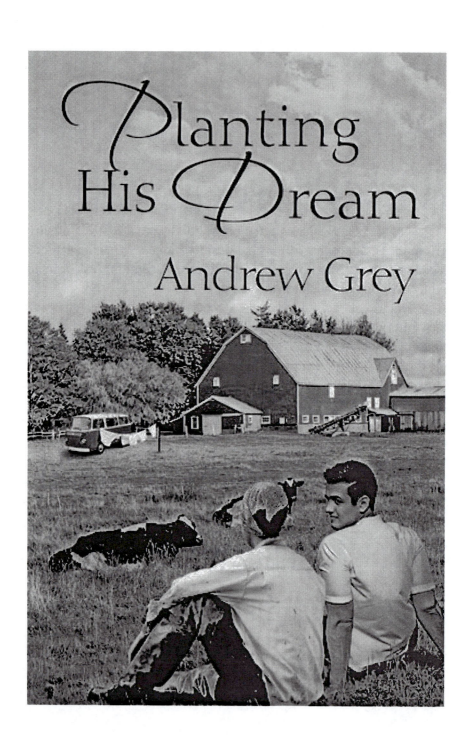

Foster dreams of getting away, but after his father's death, he has to take over the family dairy farm. It soon becomes clear his father hasn't been doing the best job of running it, so not only does Foster need to take over the day-to-day operations, he also needs to find new ways of bringing in revenue.

Javi has no time to dream. He and his family are migrant workers, and daily survival is a struggle, so they travel to anywhere they can get work. When they arrive in their old van, Foster arranges for Javi to help him on the farm.

To Javi's surprise, Foster listens to his ideas and actually puts them into action. Over days that turn into weeks, they grow to like and then care for each other, but they come from two very different worlds, and they both have responsibilities to their families that neither can walk away from. Is it possible for them to discover a dream they can share? Perhaps they can plant their own and nurture it together to see it grow, if their different backgrounds don't separate them forever.

www.dreamspinnerpress.com

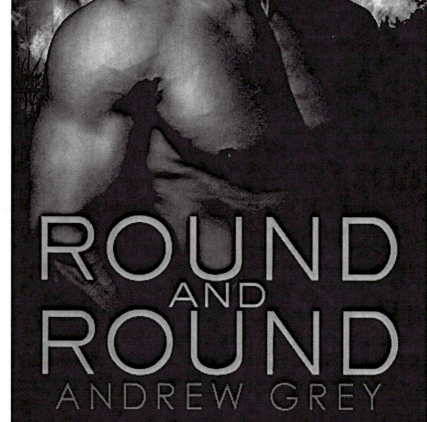

ROUND
AND
ROUND

ANDREW GREY

Sequel to *Backward*
Bronco's Boys: Book Four

When it comes to love, Kevin Foster can't seem to win. Some consider him a hero, but dousing an arsonist's attempt to burn Bronco's to the ground puts Kevin on the vengeful criminal's radar. Afterward, the arsonist fixates on Kevin, determined to burn away every part of Kevin's life.

Coming to Kevin's rescue more than once, and in more ways than one, is "MacDreamy Hotness"—firefighter Angus MacTavish. Not only is Angus smitten at first sight, he learns Kevin's nickname for him, intriguing him further.

When Angus discovers Kevin is the arsonist's target, he takes it upon himself to protect him at any cost. Soon Kevin works his way into a heart Angus thought he'd closed off for good. Things heat up between them, but the arsonist has no intention of letting Kevin finally find happiness. Hopefully Angus and Kevin can stop him before he reduces everything Kevin values to ash—including the love igniting between him and Angus.

www.dreamspinnerpress.com

CPSIA information can be obtained
at www.ICGtesting.com
Printed in the USA
LVOW10s0925210517
535244LV00029B/495/P